QUICK TAP

A SPICY RUGBY ROMANCE NOVELLA

C(R)OUCH BIND SET SERIES
BOOK 0.5

HEIDI STARK

COPYRIGHT

IMPORTANT NOTE

Unlike some of my other books, this one doesn't include an encyclopedia full of trigger warnings.

However, it does contain:

- graphic sex

- mention of serious illness of a family member (not specified)

To the dirty-talking strangers
who become the ghosts we can't shake
the memories we can't erase,
and the standards no one else can meet.

Sometimes the best plays are the ones
that leave marks on your skin.
May you find someone who ruins you
in all the ways that matter.

CHAPTER 1

DYLAN

THE PAST

grip the bench so hard my fingers ache, nails pressing half-moons into my palms. My cleats tap against the ground, restless, itching to move, to do something. I can see the game unraveling in front of me, and it's killing me.

We're losing ground. Fast.

I see the gaps in our defense before they even open, the missed tackles, the plays I could have executed better. I know what needs to be done. But instead of being out there, making a difference, I'm stuck here, watching it all fall apart.

Kat shifts beside me, arms crossed so tight it looks like she's holding herself back from throwing something. Her voice is sharp, bitter. "This is bullshit, Dyl."

I don't answer, because what's the point? We both know why I'm on the bench.

It's not because I'm not good enough.

It's not because I haven't earned it.

It's because I'm not one of his favorites.

Our coach barely glances my way. He sticks with the players he's comfortable with, the ones who've been here longer, the ones who get the benefit of the doubt no matter how many times they fuck up.

I train harder. I play sharper. I have the stats to prove it. But none of that matters when the person making the calls refuses to see me.

Another turnover. Another missed tackle. I squeeze my fists tighter. If I were out there, I'd have made that stop. I'd have been in position. I could have changed the game.

Instead, I sit.

Fuming.

Waiting.

Hoping for something that might never come.

———

The second half is slipping away when it happens.

A brutal hit—mistimed, reckless. One of our starters goes down, clutching her knee, her face twisted in agony. The medic runs onto the field, signaling for a sub.

My breath catches.

This is it.

I know I should be next in line. But the coach hesitates.

He scans the bench, looking for a way around putting me in. Like maybe, if he stares long enough, another option will magically appear.

Kat tenses beside me. "Are you serious?" she mutters under her breath.

Then, finally—reluctantly—his gaze lands on me.

"Porter. Get in."

I'm on my feet before he finishes speaking, sprinting onto the field, muscles already firing, body snapping into motion.

I don't just play—I take over.

I find the space, carve through defenders, fire off a clean, sharp pass that sets up a try. A minute later, I land a tackle so hard the opposing player stumbles on the replay.

The shift is immediate. The momentum flips. The team rallies.

By the final whistle, we've fought our way back.

I'm breathless, sweat dripping down my temple, my heart pounding so hard I can feel it in my teeth. I did exactly what I knew I could do.

I look for him. The coach.

I expect… something. A nod. A finally. An acknowledgment that I should have been in the game from the start.

Instead, he just shrugs. "Right place, right time."

Like it was luck.

Like it wasn't inevitable.

The words hit harder than any tackle.

No credit. No recognition. No apology for leaving me on the bench when I should have been leading from the field.

And in that moment, I know—some people will never see me for what I am. No matter how hard I fight.

The past lingers in the back of my mind as I think about the new training facility.

Everything there is pristine, from what I've read. High-tech recovery rooms, a gym packed with state-of-the-art equipment, a training field so perfect it looks like something out of a sports documentary.

The coaches were so nice over Zoom, their smiles warm, their words full of promise.

It *feels* different.

It *should* be different.

But I can't shake the fear.

What if this is just another version of the same story? What if the head coach already has his favorites? What if I get there, work my ass off, *proving* myself over and over again, only to be overlooked when it matters most?

I'll make sure to watch the assistant coaches during drills, searching their faces for the same indifference I've seen before.

Every correction, every comment, every glance will probably feel like a test.

Will they pay attention? Will they *actually* see me?

Or am I already being slotted into the background?

That's if they accept me at all.

I'll need to push harder. Run faster. Play sharper.

And still, paranoia gnaws at me. *Is this real? Or am I making myself crazy?*

During a virtual happy hour to meet some of the current team, one of the veterans—Ana—grins. "You'll be great. You've got nothing to prove."

I force a smile.

But she's wrong.

Because I *do*.

I always will.

As I disembark the plane, my breath steady, my muscles thrumming, I make myself a silent promise—*I will not let them bench me again.*

CHAPTER 2

DYLAN

The wheels of my duffel bag rattle across the pavement, the sound too loud in the early morning quiet. I tighten my grip on the handle, rolling my shoulders back, forcing myself to stand taller. The professional rugby training facility looms ahead—sleek, massive, a fortress of glass and steel.

This is it. Everything I've worked toward.

So why does it feel like I'm walking into enemy territory?

I exhale, reminding myself why I'm here.

This is the next step.

I belong here.

I've trained for this.

The words loop through my head like a mantra, but a tiny voice in the back of my mind isn't convinced.

A group of players pass nearby, chatting, their laughter easy and familiar. One of them glances my way—then does a quick second look.

I know exactly why.

My hair.

Even without a mirror, I know exactly how obnoxiously vibrant it looks in the daylight.

Half of it is bright magenta—loud, rebellious, unapologetic. The other half? Teal, bold and electric. It's like I dipped my head in vivid paint—the two bold shades I haven't decided if I love or regret are impossible to ignore. The contrast is sharp, the part running perfectly down the center.

It hangs just past my shoulders, straight but slightly messy, the kind of half-styled, half-chaotic look that makes it obvious I don't usually spend much time fixing it—or in this case, that I just got off a plane.

I tug at the ends instinctively, feeling the weight of the color, the attention it's pulling.

Was this a mistake?

I dyed it before I left, on a whim, telling myself it was about confidence, about stepping into something new. But now, under the bright daylight, in front of a bunch of strangers who don't know me yet?

I feel like a neon sign screaming LOOK AT ME.

Great. First impression: *Reckless idiot.*

I shove my free hand in my pocket, trying not to fidget. It's fine. I've already proven myself on the field. That's what matters.

At the entrance, a team rep—mid-40s, clipboard in hand—waits just inside. She gives me a polite but professional nod.

"Dylan Porter?"

"That's me," I say, forcing a confident tone.

"Welcome. Here's your itinerary for the visit. She hands me a printed schedule, then gestures for me to follow her.

The tour begins in the locker rooms. Rows of pristine lockers, benches, the scent of fresh laundry mixed with that underlying permanent sweat smell every rugby facility has. I clock where the women's section is, mentally placing where I'll be changing.

Then the place I care about most—the training field. Players are already out there running drills, shouting plays, moving with a sharpness that makes my pulse spike.

The gym & rehab area are massive, with more weights and state-of-the-art equipment than I've ever had access to. A few players nod in my direction, but most stay focused, lifting, stretching, rehabbing injuries.

I should be soaking this all in. Instead, I feel antsy. My hands are still in my pockets, itching to move, to do something other than follow and nod.

"We're excited to see what you can do tomorrow," the rep says as we finish the tour.

I nod, throwing on an easy, confident smile—the kind I use when I need to fake certainty. "Can't wait," I say. But my stomach tightens.

A few players linger near the entrance, their conversation halting as I approach. I recognize the moment—the subtle sizing up of a newcomer.

One of them, a tall woman with an easy, welcoming smile, steps forward first.

"Dylan, right? Welcome. I'm Ana." She offers her hand, and I shake it, feeling some of the tension in my chest ease.

Not everyone is so quick to be friendly.

A second player, lean and sharp-eyed, watches me like she's waiting to be impressed before she bothers saying much.

A third barely glances my way before muttering something to a teammate, her eyes flicking to my hair.

Awesome. Already standing out for the wrong reason.

One of them—a guy about my height, solid build, messy curls—grins as he nods toward my hair. "So, the hair—what's the story?"

I knew this was coming.

I could play it off, say it was intentional. A statement. A power move.

But the truth?

It was an impulse. Something I did at home before I left, maybe to distract myself from nerves.

Instead of over-explaining, I shrug, keeping it casual. "Just felt like a change."

No one pushes further, but I can tell some of them are already forming opinions.

Fine. Let them.

They'll figure out soon enough—I'm not here to stand out for my hair. I'm here to win.

As I head toward my assigned locker, I glance back at the training field one more time.

Tomorrow, I prove I belong here.

No distractions.

No doubts.

No regrets.

That's the plan, anyway.

But deep down, I have a feeling—this is just the beginning.

CHAPTER 3

DYLAN

The longer I walk through the halls of this place, the smaller I feel.

When I first arrived, I was excited. Confident. Ready. But now? Now, I'm wondering if I was just lying to myself.

This isn't like my old club. Everyone here is good.

Not just good—razor-sharp, their movements instinctive, fluid, practiced. I catch glimpses of them in the gym, lifting with perfect form. On the field, their footwork is unreal, their timing precise. They move like they already know what the others are going to do before it happens.

A well-oiled machine.

And me? *I'm the new piece that might not fit.*

My steps slow slightly as the tour continues. No one else notices, but I do.

I was supposed to come in confident, ready to dominate. But the longer I watch, the more I start questioning—am I fast enough for this? Is my passing game as clean as I thought? What if I'm just some impulsive idiot who dyed her hair bright colors and thought she could keep up with professionals?

I clench my fists, trying to push the thoughts down.

If I let myself spiral now, I'll psych myself out before I even have a chance to get an offer.

I try to focus as the rep finishes the tour, rattling off information about schedules, training expectations, club rules.

I nod at the right times, and try to act like I'm absorbing it all. But my head is spinning, and not from the overload of details.

It's the pressure.

It's the fact that I have no idea if I'm a good fit.

I shove my hands into my pockets as we walk through the last part of the facility, my stomach twisting.

What if I made a huge mistake coming here?

I've never doubted myself like this before. Rugby is the one thing I've always been sure about. But standing in a facility full of players who already know their place, know their strengths, know each other—I feel like an outsider.

Like I'm one misstep away from proving I don't belong.

As soon as the tour wraps up, I head outside, needing to breathe.

The crisp air fills my lungs, and I exhale slowly, rolling my shoulders.

I need to snap out of this.

I need to pull my head out of my ass before I let self-doubt choke me before I even have a chance to step onto the field.

I dig my phone out of my pocket and scroll to the name I need—my best friend and roommate, Kat.

It only rings once before she picks up.

"Hey, loser."

A snort. "You call me at this time and I'm the loser?"

"You were probably sitting on your ass doing nothing."

"Excuse you, I was deeply invested in a show that requires my full emotional attention."

"Oh, you mean you're not waiting to watch the latest *Love is Blind* episodes with me?"

"You caught me," she confesses. "But I'll rewatch with you. No spoilers, I promise."

I huff out a laugh, the tension in my chest loosening slightly.

This is why I called.

But of course, Kat doesn't let it slide. Her voice shifts slightly, more serious. "Okay, spill. What's going on?"

I hesitate. I don't want to say it out loud. Because if I say it, it's real. But I also know she won't let me off the hook. I grip the phone tighter, my voice quieter than before. "What if I don't belong here?"

No hesitation on her end. "You're overthinking again, aren't you?"

I sigh. "Maybe."

"Dylan. Shut up."

I snort. "Wow, thanks. That was inspiring."

"I'm serious."

There's a long pause, then Kat's voice softens slightly. "You're one of the best players I know. You're going to crush it."

I press my lips together. I want to believe that. "Yeah... but what if I don't?"

"Then you'll figure it out. But you didn't fly all the way there to doubt yourself. You didn't get here by accident. You worked your ass off for this. You earned it."

Her words hit deep.

"Everyone second-guesses themselves," she continues. "But you? You don't quit."

I exhale slowly, staring out at the empty section of the training field in front of me.

"I've watched you take hits that would break other people and get up like it was nothing," she says. "So what's different now?"

"This is different," I admit. "It feels like I'm out of my league. *Way* out of my league. This is the real deal. It's a step too far."

"No, it's not," Kat counters. "It's just another game. You can either let your head screw you over, or you can walk onto that field tomorrow and do what you always do—kick ass."

My heart pounds. Because deep down, I know she's right. "But what if I mess up?"

"Then you get back up. Like you always do."

A slow smile tugs at my lips.

"You make it sound so simple."

"It is". I can almost hear her shrugging through the phone. "You just like making things harder than they need to be."

I roll my eyes. "You're annoying."

"You love me."

I don't realize how much lighter my chest feels until I hang up.

I stare at the field in front of me, my fingers loosening around my phone. The doubt is still there, but it's quieter now. I'm still nervous. Still unsure of what's coming next. But one thing is crystal clear—I'm not giving up before I even try.

No distractions.

No impulsive mistakes.

No self-doubt getting in the way.

Tomorrow, I walk onto that field and prove I belong here.

And if I fall?

I'll get back up.

Like I always do.

CHAPTER 4

KAI

The message comes in just after midnight.

Mum's appointment went okay. Docs say we wait and see.

I stare at the words, rereading them as if they'll change. As if they'll suddenly mean something better. *Wait and see.* What the hell does that even mean?

My jaw tightens, thumb hovering over the keyboard. I should say something. Ask for details. Call my brother and actually hear his voice instead of just reading cold, blue text on a screen.

Instead, I just sit there, phone burning in my hand, because I don't know what the fuck I'm supposed to say.

Sorry I'm not there? Sorry I'm selfish? Sorry I left you all to deal with this while I chase a dream that was never meant for me?

I drag a hand down my face and exhale hard, staring at the ceiling. I should be home. *I should be there.* Instead, I'm in a high-rise apartment on the other side of the world, my body still aching from today's match, my fridge full of food I barely touch, my career looking better than ever while my family holds it together without me.

I type out a response.

Sweet as. Let me know if she needs anything.

I delete it.

I try again.

How's she really doing?

Delete.

I settle on a thumbs-up emoji and send it before I can think too hard. A coward's response.

My phone screen dims, the message thread still open. I should follow up. Call Mum. Let her hear my voice, let her know I still give a shit.

Instead, I set the phone down, press my fingers to my temples, and breathe through the guilt clawing up my throat.

New Zealand. The academy.

I can still smell the damp grass, the sweat, the adrenaline. The way the floodlights turned the field into a spotlight at night, the whole world narrowing to just this game, just this chance.

Make the play. Get noticed. Prove you belong here.

Every practice, I went harder. Stayed longer. Studied tape until I could see it playing behind my eyelids when I tried to sleep. I chased every edge I could get.

And for a while, it felt like enough.

Until it wasn't.

The All Blacks never called.

I waited. Told myself *next* selection cycle, *next* tournament, *next* season. But deep down, I already knew.

I wasn't exceptional.

I was a great player, sure. Good enough to start. Good enough to dominate in club rugby. But that's all I'd ever be—*good enough.*

Not *the best.*

Not *the kind of player they build teams around.*

I watched others move past me—faster, sharper, younger. They weren't working harder than me. They weren't *hungrier.* They were just *better.*

And I had to sit with that. Had to swallow the slow realization that I'd never wear the black jersey. Never be a name people spoke about in hushed, reverent tones.

So, I did the next best thing. I played club rugby. I won. A lot. It stopped feeling like an accomplishment after a while. The fire inside me dulled, match after match, win after win.

And then, I got an offer.

An overseas contract. More money. A higher level of competition. A new start.

It was the smart move. It was the *only* move.

But it still felt like failure.

I sat across from Mum at the kitchen table, the offer letter folded neatly in front of me. I didn't know why I brought it. She didn't need to read it to know what it said.

She smiled, soft and proud. *"I always knew you'd leave, baby. Go show them what you can do."*

But when I looked at Dad, all I saw was the quiet weight of disappointment.

He didn't say much. Didn't argue. Just nodded once and kept eating.

I told myself it was fine. That I didn't need his approval. That I was making the right call.

Still, as I packed my bags, as I booked my flight, as I said my goodbyes, I couldn't shake the feeling that I was running away.

————

The music is loud, the bar packed with bodies, my teammates in high spirits. Someone shoves a fresh beer into my hand, claps me on the back.

"Feels good, huh?"

I nod. Force a grin. Lift the drink like I'm actually part of this celebration.

But my mind is a thousand miles away.

All I can think about is Mum standing in the kitchen back

home, stirring a pot of something warm, too tired to eat it. Dad working late shifts, the same way he always has. My brother—my kid brother—shouldering responsibilities I left behind.

My life is here now. I should be grateful. I *am* grateful. But every win, every highlight reel moment, every paycheck with too many zeros just makes the guilt sit heavier.

Am I even *allowed* to be happy here?

I pull out my phone. Scroll back to my brother's message.

Mum's appointment went okay. Docs say we wait and see.

I type:

I'm sorry.

I stare at the words for a long time. Then, before I can overthink it, I delete them.

And I don't send anything at all.

CHAPTER 5

DYLAN

THE NEXT MORNING

step onto the training field, my cleats pressing into the damp grass, and my stomach twists like it's trying to eat itself.

This is it.

Coaches are watching.

Potential future teammates are watching.

Every single set of eyes on me, waiting to see if I'll crack under pressure.

I pull in a deep breath, rolling out my shoulders as the assistant coach steps forward, clipboard in hand. His gaze sweeps over the team, pausing on me for half a second before he starts talking.

"We'll be running a full-speed scrimmage today. Two teams. No holding back."

He doesn't have to spell it out. This is a test.

"We want to see how you handle real-time play against a professional squad."

I already know the stakes.

This is the moment I prove I belong—or I don't.

If I fuck this up, I'll spend the rest of my time here playing catch-up, trying to claw my way back into the coaches' good graces.

No pressure or anything.

The game starts at full intensity. No warm-up, no easing into it—just a whistle and immediate chaos.

I react on instinct, rushing forward as my team spreads out. The ball moves fast—*too* fast.

This isn't like playing with my regular squad. We're not bad, but here, it's different—the passes are clean, effortless, the movement fluid, practiced. They know each other's rhythms. They anticipate plays before they even happen. And I feel like I'm half a second behind.

The ball comes my way, and I catch it easily—but my next move? Hesitation.

I don't see the best passing lane immediately, and that split-second of doubt nearly gets my pass intercepted.

A warning bell rings in my head. *Too slow.*

A second later, an opposing player cuts past me, and I move in for a tackle, but she sidesteps, leaving me grasping at air.

Shit.

"Push up, Porter!" someone yells from behind me.

I grit my teeth and reset, but I can feel it. The doubt.

Am I actually ready for this?

I can't do this.

I can't hesitate.

I block out the noise and force my mind to focus on the game, not the pressure.

The next time I get the ball—I don't hesitate.

I see the opening.

I cut through the gap.

A defender slams into me, but I keep driving forward.

I absorb the hit, my feet digging into the turf as I fight for space. The moment I feel a second defender closing in, I flip a quick pass to my teammate. Clean. Sharp. Precise.

And just like that, something clicks. I start seeing the field differently. Instead of reacting late, I start anticipating. I watch the way my teammates move, the way the defense shifts. I track the ball's momentum, feeling the rhythm of play instead of chasing it.

The next time a pass comes my way, I don't think—I move. I sprint into open space, cut inside, and call for it. The ball comes fast, but I catch it cleanly, pivot, and fire a pass wide before a defender can close me down.

The pace is still brutal, but I'm adjusting. I'm in it now. The game keeps moving, and so do I.

Then, a moment presents itself—a massive tackle opportunity. One of the opposing team's best players breaks through the defensive line, her eyes locked on the try zone. I see it happening a second before anyone else.

Go.

I charge. Time slows for a split second. I plant my feet, lower my body, and slam into her. The impact shakes through my bones, but I don't let go. We hit the ground hard, the ball popping loose.

For a heartbeat, the field goes silent. Then, from the sideline —"Hell of a hit, Porter!"

My pulse hammers in my ears as I push myself up, breath ragged. The doubt? Gone. Confidence surges through me.

I stop thinking about not messing up and start playing to win. I start calling plays, directing movement—even though I'm new, even though I know some of these players weren't sure about me.

And they start listening.

The next time I get the ball, I see the defense pressing up fast —so I do something unexpected. Instead of running or passing short, I step back and send a long, pinpoint kick-pass across the field. The ball drops perfectly into my teammate's hands on the wing. She bolts for the try zone, crossing the line untouched. The sideline erupts. Even the players who were skeptical when I first walked onto the field? They're paying attention now.

We're in the last few minutes. I see another opening—one that requires me to take the risk myself. The ball swings my way, and I don't hesitate. I cut through the defense, pushing into open space.

Two defenders rush in.

I fake left. Spin right. Break free. Full sprint now, nothing but the try line ahead. My lungs burn, but I don't stop. I dive over the line, grounding the ball just as the whistle blows.

Game over.

And me?

I fucking did it.

I walk off the field, my legs heavy, body bruised, my heart pounding with adrenaline.

Someone claps me on the back—a veteran player who barely acknowledged me before.

"Didn't think you had it in you," she says. "Guess I was wrong."

The assistant coach steps in next. "You were good in your scouting games. Today? You were even better. Don't see many hookers who can run like that."

I nod, still catching my breath.

"Keep playing like that," he says, "and you'll make a real impact here."

I barely contain the rush of relief. I proved myself.

Not just to them—but to *me.*

As I head toward the locker room, one thought stays with me.

I can do this.

CHAPTER 6

KAI

The roar of the crowd is deafening.

Floodlights glare down on the pitch, casting long shadows across the turf, illuminating the sweat-slicked bodies of my teammates as we collide in the final moments of play.

The scoreboard flashes. We're winning. *Dominating.*

I should feel it. The rush. The fire in my veins. The satisfaction that comes with knowing we controlled every phase, crushed every play, left the opposition scrambling in our wake.

Instead, it feels... *hollow.*

I push forward, reading the gaps in the other team's defense. The ball comes to me, smooth and effortless, and I make the break, slicing through defenders like they aren't even there. My body moves on instinct—duck, step, surge forward—but my mind?

My mind is *a thousand miles away.*

Mum's sick and it could be really serious.

I shouldn't be here.

A body slams into me, jolting me back to the present. I absorb the hit, roll off, and push up fast, the ball still secure in my hands. I hear the crash of bodies behind me, the grunt of effort, but none of it *sticks*.

I get the offload away, and seconds later, we score.

The crowd erupts. My teammates slap my back, a rough mix of celebration and adrenaline-fueled aggression, but it barely registers.

It's another win. Another moment where I'm supposed to *feel* something.

But all I can think about is my mum sitting in that too-small waiting room appointment after appointment, flipping through old magazines, waiting for a doctor to tell her if the cells in her body are killing her or if she's got more time.

A whistle blows. Full-time. The game is ours.

I run a hand through my damp hair, my chest rising and falling with steady, controlled breaths. Around me, my team celebrates. Laughter. Cheers. Grins stretched across sweaty faces.

I should be happy. I should be proud.

Instead, I feel like a fucking ghost in my own body.

I glance at the stands out of habit, like I expect to see my mum there. Like I haven't been gone for years now.

She'd always come to my matches when I was younger. She was the loudest one there, standing in the front row, clapping like every tackle I made, every try I scored, was the greatest thing she'd ever seen.

I should be there for *her* now.

Instead, I'm here. Chasing something that doesn't even feel real anymore.

Someone claps a hand on my shoulder.

"Solid game, bro," one of the guys says, his grin wide, his body still humming with post-match adrenaline. "You carved them up."

I force a nod. A smirk that doesn't quite reach my eyes.

"Yeah," I say. "Cheers."

I turn away before he can see through the bullshit.

The locker room is loud—music blasting, guys still high off the win. I sit at my locker, elbows on my knees, my head dropped forward.

On instinct, I grab my phone out of my bag and read my brother's message from yesterday.

Wait and see.

A sharp pang slices through me.

I should be there. I should have been sitting next to her in that waiting room, asking the questions she never will, making sure they're doing *everything* they can.

Instead, I was here. On this field. Winning a game that doesn't even matter.

My fingers hover over my screen. I type:

Wish I could've been there.

I delete it.

I try again:

Let me know if she needs anything.

Delete.

Finally, I send nothing.

I just sit there, staring at the floor, my jaw clenched so tight it aches.

Outside, my team celebrates. The crowd filters out. The stadium lights begin to dim.

And me?

I sit in the silence, feeling the weight of all the miles between me and home.

CHAPTER 7

DYLAN

By the time I step out of the locker room, my brain feels like it's been wrung dry.

The day has been a whirlwind—more introductions and drills, another tour, overanalyzing every single interaction. My muscles ache from the scrimmage, and my head is buzzing with everything I learned.

My original plan is to go back to my hotel. Shower. Eat something simple. Get my mind right. Smart choices. No distractions.

Then I hear it—"Hey, Porter! You coming to dinner?"

I blink, turning toward the voice. A group of players—some of the ones I met earlier, some I haven't spoken to yet—are standing by the entrance, clearly waiting for my answer.

For a second, I hesitate. This was not in my plan. I was going to lay low. Rest. Keep my focus.

But then I remember my friend's pep talk—"You can either let your head screw you over, or you can walk onto that field tomorrow and do what you always do—kick ass." And I did. The hard work is done.

And really—blowing off steam doesn't mean losing control,

right? It's just dinner. It's a chance to build some connections, maybe actually relax for the first time today. And I don't want to get labeled as the antisocial new girl who thinks she's too good for team bonding. So I shove my hands into my pockets, smirk, and say, "Why not?"

———

The place they take me is casual but packed, the kind of spot that screams team favorite. Long wooden tables, a low hum of music, and the walls are lined with signed jerseys and old team photos.

Dylan Porter, welcome to the inner circle.

I know it's just a test drive, but it still feels good to be included. The worry about whether I'd belong here feels like a distant memory.

I take a seat near the middle of the group, at first just listening as they talk around me. They discuss the program—

"Training is brutal, but worth it." Then the coaches— "They'll push you until you feel like you're dying, but then you realize you're the strongest you've ever been." Then the competition—"Some of the returning players are scary good. You'll see."

I nod along, absorbing everything, still feeling a little like an outsider looking in.

Then—"Okay, I gotta ask."

I glance up as one of the women—tall, lean, eyes sharp with curiosity—leans across the table, smirking.

Oh no. Here it comes—really, what the hell was I thinking? I came to leave my mark on rugby and this is all anyone is concerned about.

"What's with the hair? We thought you were into cosplay or something when we first saw you. Rumors were swirling that Harley Quinn herself had arrived on campus."

For a beat, I just blink.

Then laughter erupts around the table. Even some of the ones who were cooler toward me earlier are cracking up.

I grin despite myself. "Yeah, no. Sorry to disappoint. Just an impulse decision."

One of them nudges my shoulder. "Damn. So no secret anime alter ego?"

I smirk. "Not unless rugby counts as a fantasy world."

More laughter. And just like that, the energy shifts completely.

As the meal goes on, I find myself talking more.

Sharing a little about where I came from, what drew me to rugby, and what I want from this opportunity.

I expect them to just nod and move on, but instead, they listen and ask real questions. Before my on-field performance today, they were sizing me up like competition. Now? They're actually taking me seriously. It's a subtle shift, but a big one.

And for the first time today, I don't feel like I'm on the outside looking in.

Plates are cleared. Drinks are finished.

Then someone leans back in their chair, stretching. "Alright, so who's up for a drink?"

A few heads turn toward me. "We usually hit up a bar nearby after training kicks our asses. It's tradition."

I hesitate. I already pushed myself by saying yes to dinner. I already stepped out of my comfort zone. I should go back. Rest. Stay smart.

But something about tonight feels different. I glance at my reflection in the restaurant's window. The bright colors in my hair catch the light. And instead of feeling self-conscious about it, I feel bold.

I meet my teammates' expectant stares. I grin. "Alright. One drink."

The cheers that go up are loud enough to turn heads in the restaurant.

I laugh, shaking my head as they start plotting where we're going.

When we leave the restaurant, I head back to my hotel first—

because if I'm doing this, I'm doing it right. I put on a cute outfit that's a little out of my normal wardrobe choice—a short flared skirt with a matching crop top. I add more makeup than normal —sharp cat's-eye liner and a bold red lipstick. I own the version of me I saw in that window reflection.

Because maybe—just maybe—tonight isn't just about proving myself on the field.

Maybe it's about letting myself be seen.

And for once?

That doesn't feel like a bad thing.

CHAPTER 8

DYLAN

The rooftop bar's neon sign casts a vibrant glow over the sidewalk as we approach. The electric hum of bass-heavy music pulses from inside, deep enough to vibrate in my chest.

I'm already out of my element. But for once? I don't mind.

The elevator ride up is packed with bodies—teammates, strangers, people laughing, buzzing with energy. When the doors slide open, the full weight of the club crashes over me.

The music. The lights. The scent of sweat, spilled liquor, and expensive cologne.

It's chaotic, overwhelming, alive.

I scan the space, taking it in. In the center, a massive dance floor, pulsing with bodies, the beat commanding every movement. A sleek bar stretching along the back wall, lined with glassware that catches the club lights. Booths tucked into the corners, occupied by groups leaning in over drinks, laughter spilling into the air.

So this is where they all unwind.

Teammates scatter immediately—some heading straight for the bar, others already pulling each other onto the dance floor.

I lean against a railing near the edge of the floor, soaking it in. I've never been much for clubbing. The noise, the crowd, the artificial heat of too many bodies in one place—But tonight? It feels electric.

The music isn't just sound—it's something I feel in my bones. The lights blur, colors melting together in a way that makes everything seem more alive.

I don't feel like an outsider tonight.

Maybe I should go out more.

Movement at the far side of the club draws my attention. Not the dance floor—past that. Toward the VIP section near the bar. A cluster of women crowds around a single stool.

I notice him immediately. Broad shoulders. That unmistakable rugby build—powerful, athletic. Tanned brown skin, inked with tribal tattoos curling over his forearms and biceps. A cocky, half-lidded smile that says he already knows exactly how this night is going to play out.

I don't need to be close to know—he's enjoying the attention.

But not in a way that feels genuine.

More like... he's letting it happen. Like this is routine for him.

I watch, half-amused, half-fascinated, as the women around him seem to move in constant rotation.

A blonde in a skintight dress leans in first, whispering something in his ear.

He grins, nods, and murmurs something back that makes her giggle.

Then, almost on cue, she shifts and a brunette in red slides into her place, her hand resting lightly on his knee. She tilts her head, pouting slightly, like she's repeating the same move as the first girl.

He barely reacts. Same grin. Same murmur. Same giggle.

A third woman, this one with dark curls and sharp cat-eye

makeup, swoops in next, handing him a fresh drink before smoothly replacing the brunette's position.

He accepts the glass with lazy, easy charm.

Like he's done this a hundred times before.

The first blonde reappears, apparently not happy about being rotated out. She nudges the brunette.

The brunette nudges the third girl.

And suddenly, they're locked in some sort of silent, passive-aggressive battle for position.

The guy just leans back, amused but completely unbothered.

I can't help it. I laugh under my breath, shaking my head.

So that's the game he plays.

I've seen guys like him before—the ones who never have to chase. The ones who attract attention without even trying. The ones who can say three words and make someone melt.

Good for him, I guess.

But there's zero chance he'd ever be interested in me.

I'm not the type to fawn.

I'm not here for this kind of attention.

And honestly?

I'd rather compete against him on the field than play that game.

With that thought, I shrug him off completely, turning back toward the bar—unaware that Kai has just caught sight of me.

CHAPTER 9

KAI

The world around me blurs together in flashing lights and laughter.

The bass thrums beneath my feet, a constant, steady pulse. The liquor is smooth, the attention is effortless, and the women? They come and go in an easy, predictable rhythm.

One leans in, whispering something against my ear. Her perfume is strong, her voice is sweet, practiced. I don't register a single word she says.

Doesn't matter. *I already know the script.*

It's a game I've long since mastered. Playful smirks. Brushed fingers. The push-pull of waiting for me to make the move they want.

It's a distraction. A habit.

A routine that feels emptier every time I go through the motions.

At least it keeps me from thinking too much about what's going on back home.

At least it's easy. Or at least, it was.

Because then something shifts.

I barely register the woman against me anymore. My grin remains in place, but my focus has already left the conversation.

A presence at the bar catches my attention.

I don't know her name yet. But I know immediately—she's not like the rest of them.

She's with a group of women, but she's not clawing for attention. She's laughing, but it's not that saccharine, flirty kind I hear every night in places like this.

It's real. *Effortless.*

The kind of laugh that lights up her whole face.

She's wearing a matching crop top and skirt, nothing particularly scandalous, yet I can't stop looking.

And then there's the hair. Bright. Unexpected. A little chaotic. It should clash, but somehow, it fits her perfectly.

I tilt my head slightly, studying her. She's confident without trying. Not performing. Not seeking approval.

She's not trying to be seen.

Which, ironically, makes it impossible to look away.

She leans in to talk to one of her friends, completely unaware of how she moves. There's a natural grace to her, a sharp control in every motion.

An athlete.

Her stance isn't delicate—it's grounded. Balanced. Unshakable.

The other women in this club? Most of them want to be noticed. Want to be desired.

Her? She isn't even playing the game.

I wait.

Most women have looked at me by now. It's a pattern. A rhythm. A dance I know too well.

But her? Not once. Not even that subtle flick of the eyes most women do when they're pretending not to look.

I give it a few seconds.

A full minute.

Still nothing.

A slow, amused smirk tugs at my lips.

Interesting.

It's not just that she hasn't looked. It's that she hasn't once given off the energy of someone trying not to look.

Most women who pretend not to notice me are still hyper-aware of my presence. They'll angle their shoulders just right. They'll play with their hair, shift their stance, wait for me to notice them first. They want me to chase. It's part of the game.

But this woman?

She genuinely doesn't give a shit that I'm here.

And *that* is a first.

I watch as she takes a sip of her drink, still fully engaged in her group's conversation.

I wonder what her voice sounds like.

I wonder if her laugh always comes that easily.

I wonder if she's already taken?

Not interested in men?

Genuinely unaware of who I am?

The last possibility makes something slowly unfurl in my chest.

No way.

That's impossible.

She has to know.

Right?

I'm used to a very particular dynamic.

Women who seek me out.

Women who wait for me to make the first move.

Women who play the push-pull game but ultimately give in.

This?

This is new.

This is different.

This is intriguing.

I don't chase.

I don't need to.

But something about her makes me want to test the waters.

My attention shifts completely. The rest of the club fades.

The woman beside me nudges me, trying to regain my focus. "What are you looking at?"

I grin lazily, leaning back, stretching like I have all the time in the world. "Nothing."

My eyes flick back to her for a few more beats, something sharp and knowing in my gaze.

I don't have to call attention to myself.

I don't have to do anything at all.

Because sooner or later?

She's going to look.

And when she does?

I'll be ready.

CHAPTER 10

DYLAN

'm mid-conversation with one of my potential future teammates, laughing at a terrible joke about the assistant coach's obsession with ice baths.

The night feels easy. Light. I shift slightly, just enough for my gaze to sweep across the club.

And that's when it happens.

My eyes land on *him*.

The guy I vaguely noticed earlier. The one surrounded by women, effortlessly soaking up attention like he was born for it.

Up until this exact second, he was a non-factor in my night. Just another cocky athlete. Just another guy who clearly expects people to orbit him.

But now?

Now, he's looking right back.

And everything changes.

The second our eyes meet, something in me tightens. Not just in the room—in me.

I tell myself it's just a look. Just a glance across a crowded club. Just one second too long. But it doesn't feel like just anything.

His expression is calm, unreadable. But his eyes? Laser-focused. Sharp. Knowing. Like he was waiting for me to notice him. Like he's already decided something, and I'm just catching up.

I should break the stare. I should glance off, act like it means nothing. Like I'm still in control of my night.

Instead? I hold it. Longer than I mean to. Long enough for my stomach to do that annoying, traitorous flip thing.

My body shifts without permission. My fingers tighten around my drink.

What the hell?

I'm not the type to swoon over some overconfident guy in a club. I've been around athletes my whole life. But this guy?

He's not just another athlete. There's something self-assured about him. Something dangerous in the way he watches me.

Like he's already got me figured out.

Across the room, his slow smirk deepens. Then—without hesitation—he stands. Not rushed. Not uncertain. Like it's the most obvious decision he's ever made.

And my stomach tightens.

The moment he moves, the air in the VIP section shifts. And the women surrounding him? They are not pleased.

First—the blonde currently whispering in his ear? She realizes he's not listening anymore. She follows his gaze. Spots me. And immediately shoots daggers in my direction. Like I somehow violated an unspoken contract.

Next—the brunette in red? She physically tugs his arm, trying to reclaim his attention.

"Where are you going?" she whines loudly, pouting.

Without even looking at her, I see him reply over the music. "Away."

Brunette is visibly offended.

Bodycon Dress Girl? She visibly scoffs, turning to her friend. "Are you serious? Did she put a spell on him?"

Her friend, equally scandalized, looks me up and down. "I don't get it. What does she have that we don't?"

Blonde #1 speaks up. "A death wish, apparently."

Oh no, I've started something just by existing.

I don't have to be psychic to feel the sudden hostility. The sharp whispers. The glances. The mildly scandalized outrage. The entire mood of the VIP section has changed—and somehow, I'm at the center of it. Did I just start some kind of war?

But then he moves. He steps away from the couches, leaving the mini-drama behind him.

Heading straight for me.

I swear I can feel my pulse in my throat. Not just from the weight of their collective scorn, but from the way he's watching me now—like I'm the only thing in the room.

My brain says *this is a bad idea. You said no impulsive decisions tonight.*

But my body?

Oh, my body has already decided otherwise.

The eye contact is electric, making me immediately rethink my no distractions rule.

His exit from his mini harem is both funny and dramatic, with the women still fully scandalized. I should be annoyed. I should be indifferent.

Instead? I'm amused. And slightly panicked.

Because I already know— I'm in trouble.

And he knows it too.

CHAPTER 11

He stops right in front of me, standing just close enough to invade my space but not quite touching. The air between us is thick, charged, like the moment before a lightning strike.

I should ignore him. I should turn away and let him wonder. But something in his posture, the deliberate way he closed the distance between us, makes that impossible.

I tilt my head, unimpressed—or at least, trying to be. "So, you ditched your fan club." I take a slow sip of my drink, letting the ice clink against the glass. "What, did they run out of compliments?"

He grins, slow and lazy. "They weren't saying anything interesting." His voice is smooth, but his eyes? Sharp. Amused. Calculating.

A test.

I feel it immediately. A silent question lingering between us.

What are you going to do about me?

Something tightens in my stomach, but I don't let it show. I just shrug, feigning boredom. "That's a shame." I tilt my glass slightly. "Maybe if you had more to offer, they'd have found something worth talking about."

His grin widens, entertainment flickering in his gaze. "Maybe." He tilts his head slightly, like he's already mentally dissecting me. "Or maybe you just set the bar higher." His voice is low, smooth, dangerously confident.

I give him a mock-sympathetic look. "Poor thing. And here I was thinking you were used to being the center of attention."

He leans in slightly, close enough that his breath warms my skin. "I don't mind sharing—if you're looking to make me work for it."

I scoff, arching a brow. "You think I'm trying to get your attention?"

He doesn't blink, doesn't hesitate. "I think you already have it."

My pulse kicks up, but I keep my face unreadable. "What a tragedy." I sigh dramatically, swirling the drink in my glass. "And here I was just trying to enjoy my drink, until you strolled on over here and inserted yourself into my evening."

He glances at my drink, then back at me, smirking. "You don't strike me as the kind of girl who drinks something weak."

I shrug, unfazed. "I don't strike you as anything. You don't know me."

He steps closer, voice dropping into something darker, smoother. "Not yet."

The air between us changes. The music, the crowd, the entire club fades into the background. It's just me and him. Locked in. Neither of us looking away.

I tilt my head slightly, pretending to consider something. "Is this your thing?" My voice is light, teasing, but deliberate. "Lock eyes with a girl, make her think she's special, and hope she melts before you even have to try?"

He chuckles, shaking his head slowly. "You tell me—are you melting?"

I hate that my skin is warm. That I feel off-balance. But I refuse to let him see it. "Not even close."

His smirk deepens, gaze flicking over me like he already knows the truth. "Shame." He exhales, amusement curling in his voice. "I was just starting to enjoy myself."

Fine. Let's see how he *handles it.*

I step forward this time, stepping into his space. Looking up at him, I let my voice drop just slightly. "Let me guess—you're used to women falling all over you, huh?"

He plays along, nodding once, slowly. "Most of them do."

"Hmm," I say, circling him slightly, dragging one finger along the edge of his sleeve. "And that works? A few smooth lines, some pretty eyes, and they just…" I snap my fingers. "Crack?"

He watches me, his expression darkening. Something flickers behind his eyes. Something that makes my stomach tighten. "Not all of them. There's the odd one immune to my charms." He leans in just a fraction. "But I can always tell the ones who will."

I smirk, looking up at him through my lashes. "And what do you see when you look at me?"

His jaw ticks. His eyes burn into mine. "Trouble."

I grin, sipping my drink slowly. "Good. I'd hate to be predictable."

CHAPTER 12

DYLAN

The atmosphere in the club has changed. I feel it like a live wire, buzzing between us, humming under my skin. The tension between me and this incredibly attractive man is thick, electric—like it's only a matter of time before one of us takes the plunge.

We're still bantering, pushing, testing, but the pull between us? Undeniable.

I refuse to let him rattle me. So instead, I tilt my head, smirking. "So, what's your deal? You just collect women like trophies, or do you actually have a personality?"

He chuckles, shaking his head. "You're awfully mouthy for someone who hasn't even beaten me at anything yet."

I raise a brow. "Oh? You think you could beat me at something?"

His smirk deepens, his eyes glinting. "I don't think—I know." Then, he shifts his stance, something playful but deliberate in his posture. "Alright, let's see if you're all talk or if you've actually got some game."

I cross my arms, intrigued. "Game?"

He gestures toward a high-top beside the bar. He places a coin in the middle of the table, ready to be flicked across the surface. "Coin rugby. First to three goals wins. You in?"

I scoff, unimpressed but definitely interested. "That's it? Childhood nostalgia instead of actual skill?"

He raises a brow. "What, scared I'll smoke you?"

I snort, already pulling up a barstool. "Please. I haven't played this since school. They put me up a grade in math, and the only available class was for kids who weren't great at math, so we spent the whole time playing coin rugby instead of learning quadratic equations. I was a champion. Don't underestimate me."

He laughs, low and rich, as he sits across from me. "I have a feeling it would be foolish to underestimate you."

I roll the coin between my fingers. "And what do I get if I win?"

He leans in, his voice smooth as silk. "Anything you want."

I laugh, shaking my head. "Anything, huh? What's the catch?"

His grin sharpens. "No catch. I'm just confident you won't win."

I take a slow step forward, challenging him. "And seeing you're wrong, *when* I win, what will you owe me?"

His eyes flick over me, amusement curling at his lips. "I think you'll find out."

Filthy thoughts run through my head as I gaze at his muscular physique and the gorgeous tattoos that wrap around his sculpted biceps. Heat licks at my spine, but I smother it quickly. "You're on, Pretty Boy."

The rules are simple. Each turn starts with three controlled pushes to maneuver the coin just over the edge of the table. Once it's hanging over, you have to flick it back to yourself and catch it cleanly. Only then can you take your shot, flicking the coin through the goalposts which are formed by the other person's fingers.

"Losers first," I say, nudging the coin toward him.

He shakes his head and chuckles, but takes the coin.

He takes the first push, guiding the coin expertly toward the edge of the table.

One.

Two.

Three.

It juts over perfectly, and he flicks it back to himself, catching it with ease. He lines up his shot, aims, and sends the coin sailing cleanly through my goalposts. "One-nil, baby."

I roll my shoulders. "Not bad. But watch and learn."

I push the coin forward—

One.

Two.

Three.

On the third nudge I get it to hang off the table's edge before flicking it back to myself. I really haven't played it since school, so it's been decades, but coin rugby is a bit like riding a bike.

The moment I catch it, I don't hesitate. I flick it fast, sending it right through his fingers. "One-one."

He just smirks. "Lucky shot. Don't get cocky."

The next round is faster, sharper. He scores again.

I narrow my eyes, focus, and even the score. Two-two.

A small crowd has formed around us by now, intrigued by our curious game, and the group leans in. It's sudden death.

I take my time, adjusting my angle, lining up the final shot. With one last flick, the coin slides cleanly through the goalposts. The bar erupts.

He leans back, exhaling as he runs a hand through his hair.

"Well, well. Guess I underestimated you."

I lift my drink, taking a slow sip, savoring his reaction. "Huh," I muse. "Guess that means I win. Looks like you owe me."

His grin falters just a little. I relish it. Then, he tilts his head, his smirk returning—slow, deliberate. "Not so fast, Trouble. You forgot to name my punishment."

I tap a finger against my chin, pretending to think. "Hmm. I could make you buy everyone a round…" I gesture at the sizable crowd around us, "but that'd be too easy."

I glance around for inspiration. "Or I could make you admit I'm better than you, but that's obvious."

He grins, watching me closely. "You done stalling, or do you need me to name my own punishment?"

I huff a laugh. "Fine. Go ahead, genius. What's your price for losing?"

He leans in, his voice dropping low, smooth and dangerous. "Easy. I owe you a night you'll never forget."

For the first time tonight, I hesitate. I wasn't expecting that. My pulse quickens, the tension between us so thick, I can't tell if it's a warning or a challenge. "A night I'll never forget?"

His lips curl, and he leans in slightly, his breath brushing my skin. "I don't make promises I can't keep."

My first instinct is to overthink. To talk myself out of this. To keep my guard up. This is just a game, right? I don't need complications.

But then something inside me makes me stop. For once, I'm going to take the plunge. For once, I'm going to say yes without second-guessing.

I meet his gaze, feeling the weight of his words settle between us. "Fine. But no funny business."

His smirk widens, his eyes glinting with satisfaction. "Oh, don't worry, there'll be nothing funny about it. You won't forget this night. I'll make sure of it."

A sharp shiver rolls down my spine. Not what I was expecting. My brain stutters for half a second. But my body? Oh, my body likes that answer way too much.

He sees it immediately. The slight parting of my lips. The way my fingers tighten on my drink. He leans in just a little closer. "Say yes, Trouble."

And I do.

CHAPTER 13

DYLAN

The moment I say I'm in, something shifts.

The tension between me and this mystery man was already thick, already pulling tight around us like an invisible rope. But now? Now, it's something else.

His smirk deepens, but there's a new intensity in his eyes—like a predator locking onto its prey. Without breaking eye contact, he nods toward the stairwell leading up. "Come on. I know a better view."

I raise an eyebrow, but my feet are already moving before I can think too hard about it. The adrenaline hums through me, a thrumming pulse beneath my skin.

He walks ahead, slow, easy, like he has all the time in the world. I follow, each step louder in my head than it should be.

I could turn back. But I won't.

The new upper-level rooftop is quieter, more intimate. The music from below is muffled, the chatter softer. The air is cooler up here, a stark contrast to the heat still curling in my veins.

I step forward, taking in the view. The city stretches out below us, lights glittering like scattered stars.

Behind me, he leans against the railing, arms crossed, watching me. That knowing smirk is still on his face. "Changed your mind yet?"

I scoff, stepping up beside him, my fingers lightly gripping the edge. "If you're looking for an out, just say so."

He chuckles, turning to face me fully. "Not a chance." His voice is low, sure, unshakable.

The way he says it sends a thrill straight down my spine.

He steps into my space. Slow. Deliberate. Not touching—but close enough to feel. His hands brush against my hips, a light tease of contact. Testing.

I should back up. Should call him out for pushing his luck. Instead, my breath catches. My body is suddenly, painfully aware of the inches between us.

His gaze drops to my mouth, and my lips tingle under his stare.. "You keep looking at my mouth," he has the audacity to say. *Hypocrite.*

My eyes narrow. My chin tilts up in mock defiance. "You wish."

He laughs, low and smooth. "Yeah. I do." He doesn't wait for permission. Doesn't need it. His hand moves to the back of my neck, his long fingers threading into my ridiculous, two-toned hair.

The first brush of his lips is slow. Teasing. A dare rather than a demand.

Heat flares in my chest before I even process what's happening.

Then he deepens it. Everything ignites. His free hand slides over my hip, pulling me closer until there's nothing between us but air and the dizzying press of our bodies.

The kiss turns hungry, fast. He tilts his head, taking more.

I give just as much back.

His teeth graze my bottom lip, and I gasp into his mouth. His grip tightens, backing me up against the railing.

Cold metal bites into my back—a sharp contrast to the heat

between us. My hands find his shoulders, his jaw, his hair—anything to anchor myself.

He's all control, all confidence. But I don't let him lead. When I bite back, he groans, his fingers dipping lower on my waist. When I pull his bottom lip between my teeth, he presses harder against me.

His mouth moves from my lips to my jaw. Then lower—along the curve of my throat, sending pleasant shivers through me. He lingers there, breathing me in, teeth scraping skin but not biting—just teasing. "You taste like trouble," he murmurs against my pulse.

I don't know if I want to pull him closer or push him away. Maybe both.

His hands skim under the hem of my top, his fingertips brushing the bare skin beneath. Not demanding. Not rushing. Just letting me feel him there. Waiting. Seeing if I stop him.

I don't. Instead, I tilt my head, giving him more access to my throat. A silent yes. My pussy clenches, and I know I'm getting very wet already even though he's barely touched me.

He exhales against my skin, his grip tightening just slightly. Like he knows exactly what he's doing to me.

The moment is too intense, too much. I let out a sharp breath. "I should probably stop this."

He smirks, lips brushing my jaw as he whispers, "Then stop."

But I don't.

He pulls back just enough to meet my gaze. His eyes are dark, searching, waiting.

A slow inhale drags into my lungs. I can still leave. I can still walk away.

But then he says, "Come with me."

And for once in my life, I don't think.

Instead, I just say, "Okay."

CHAPTER 14

The second we step outside, everything shifts. The bass of the music still vibrates through the walls behind us, but out here? It's just us. The air is cool against my heated skin, but it does nothing to cool the fire already consuming me. His grip on my wrist is firm—not tight, not demanding, just unhurried certainty. He doesn't rush. He doesn't ask if I'm sure. He already knows the answer. He leads me down a dimly lit alley, the neon club lights barely reaching us now.

The shadows feel private. Dangerous. The rough brick wall meets my back before I even register we've stopped.

His arm braces beside my head, his body heat radiating through the inches between us. I barely have time to breathe before his mouth is back on mine. Claiming. Demanding. Possessive. "You've been driving me insane all fucking night," he murmurs against my lips. His free hand slides under my skirt, his fingers teasing the sensitive skin on the inside of my thigh.

My breath catches, my pulse kicking up. But I refuse to let

him see how badly I want this. I arch into his touch, challenging. "Then do something about it."

His lips curve into something dark, wicked. "Oh, you have no idea."

Before he can take things further, I flip the script. I push him back, just slightly, breaking free just enough to drop to my knees on the uneven pavement. The gravel digs into my skin but I don't care. He curses, his head tipping back against the wall. "Fuck. You're not playing fair."

I smirk, dragging my nails lightly up his thighs before undoing his belt. "You don't strike me as a man who likes fair."

His eyes darken, something dangerous flickering in them. "No. I like winning."

I hum, my fingers brushing the hard outline of his cock. "Good. Let's see if you can keep standing." I undo his pants and lower them, followed by his boxer briefs. His cock springs free, long and girthy. "Mmm, you're not all talk, I see," I say, admiring him.

He smirks down at me.

I drag my tongue along his length, slow, teasing, before taking him deep. His sharp inhale turns into a deep, shuddering groan. His fingers thread into my hair, his grip tightening just slightly, guiding me. "Goddamn. Just like that."

I hollow my cheeks, moving faster, reveling in the way his breathing gets rougher.

"Fuck, you look so good like this. Taking me so fucking deep." His grip tightens, his hips subtly rolling forward. "More."

I can feel him starting to lose control. And just when he thinks he's got me figured out— I pull back completely. Wipe my mouth. Look up at him with a smirk. "You taste like arrogance."

He laughs, breathless. "And I bet you taste like trouble. Get up here."

Before I can blink, he hauls me up, flipping our positions. He walks me back, step by step, until my back meets the wooden fence at the end of the alley. His hands grip my thighs, hiking my skirt up. Then he kneels.

His mouth teases the sensitive skin of my inner thigh, teeth scraping just enough to make me shudder. "I've been thinking about this since you opened that smart mouth of yours." He teases my lips with his fingers.

I barely get out a reply before his tongue replaces his fingers, teasing over my clit. My hands grip the wooden slats behind me, my head tipping back. "Fuck—"

He groans into me, the vibration sending another jolt through my body. "You're so fucking wet for me."

He eats me like a man possessed. Messy. Unrelenting. Fully in control. His tongue flicks, circles, drags, teases—keeping me right on the edge but never giving me release. "I want you to come screaming my name."

My legs shake, my body already too far gone. "Then stop fucking teasing. And I don't even know your name."

He chuckles, dark and smug. "Ask nicely."

I yank his hair, breathless. "Fuck you."

"My name's Kai, by the way."

I smirk, panting. "Fuck you, Kai."

He grins against me, then gives me exactly what I need. His tongue moves faster, fingers curling inside me. And it's too much. I cry out, legs shaking as I shatter around him.

Before I even recover, he's back to standing. His mouth crashes against mine, and I taste myself on his lips.

I moan into the kiss, fingers tangling in his shirt, yanking him closer.

His hands grip my hips, spinning me around.

My palms brace against the fence.

His hand slides under my skirt again, teasing my entrance. "You ready for me? And I didn't catch your name."

I push back against him, desperate. "Quit fucking around. And that's because I didn't give it to you. Dylan, my name is Dylan."

He groans, adjusting himself. "I prefer to call you Trouble."

I hear the rustle of his wallet, the tear of a condom wrapper. And then he thrusts in deep.

I gasp, my nails digging into the fence. "Oh fuck—"

He grips my hips hard, holding me in place. "That's right. Take it, Trouble. Take all of me." He sets a brutal rhythm, each thrust knocking the breath from my lungs.

The sounds are filthy—skin slapping against skin. My whimpers and moans mixing with his deep, guttural groans.

One hand slides up my back, gripping my shoulder. Keeping me exactly where he wants me. "You feel so fucking good. You're squeezing me so goddamn tight."

I'm spiraling again, the pleasure building too fast. "Harder…"

He growls, obeying without hesitation. "You're going to come all over my big cock, aren't you?" His fingers slide between my legs, finding my clit.

He continues to thrust, and I moan as the coil continues to tighten in my core.

I shatter again, my body trembling, my voice breaking as I moan against the fence.

Kai follows seconds later, thrusting deep, groaning against my shoulder as he comes inside me.

We're both breathing hard, wrecked.

He leans forward, brushing his lips against the back of my neck.

"Fuck, Trouble."

I let out a breathless laugh, still pressed against the fence. "Yeah. That was… something."

He pulls back slightly, adjusting my skirt for me. A rare tenderness in the gesture. Then he smirks, eyes dark with something still unfinished. "We're not done yet."

I blink, still catching my breath. "No?"

He grabs my hand, pulling me toward the street. "Not even close." His voice is low, sure, promising. The night isn't over. Not by a long shot. "Come with me."

CHAPTER 15

When we step out of the alley, still breathless, still wrecked, the need for more doesn't fade. If anything, it burns hotter.

Kai's hand is still wrapped around my wrist, his grip firm but not desperate—just certain. Like he's not afraid I'll change my mind, but he wants me to know he's in control. Like he knows neither of us are close to done. "We're not done," he murmurs, his voice rough, gravel scraped.

I meet his gaze, chest still rising and falling, my body still tingling from everything he's already done to me. I should tell him I've had enough. That I've gotten my fill of him. Instead, I wipe my thumb across my bottom lip, smirking. "Then take me somewhere we can actually break shit."

Kai's grin is all teeth. "Say less."

We barely make it out of the alley before he flags a cab. The driver barely glances at us, too used to drunk couples climbing into the backseat with hands already wandering.

I sit beside him, the space between us barely an inch. But I can feel him.

His thigh presses against mine. The heat of him, the scent of sweat and sex and whatever cologne still lingers on his skin.

My pulse is still erratic, my body still pulsing from the last orgasm he pulled from me.

Kai leans in, his breath warm against my ear. "Think you'll still be mouthing off when I've got you under me?"

I tilt my head, smirking. "You're assuming I'll be underneath you at all."

He lets out a dark chuckle, his eyes gleaming under the passing streetlights. "Fuck, I like you."

The hotel lobby is a blur. Kai slaps his card on the counter, barely acknowledging the receptionist as they rattle off the room details. He's tapping his fingers against the desk, like he physically can't stand the wait.

I press up against him from behind, my fingers teasing along the waistband of his jeans, dipping lower just enough to make his muscles tense.

His jaw clenches. His fingers twitch against the desk. The second the keycard is in his hand, he grabs mine, pulling me toward the elevator.

The moment the elevator doors slide shut, he spins me around, trapping me against the mirrored wall. His mouth crashes onto mine, hungry, desperate, his body pressing against me, making me feel every inch of his need. His hands slide under my shirt, palming bare skin, his thumbs sweeping over my ribs, teasing, possessive. "I can't fucking wait to ruin you."

I bite his bottom lip, dragging my nails down his arms. "You talk a lot of shit for a man who hasn't proven himself yet."

His breathing hitches, his pupils blown wide. "You're gonna eat those words, Trouble."

The door barely clicks shut before he shoves me against it, his mouth back on mine.

Clothes start flying. My shirt? Gone in seconds. Kai's belt hits the floor. Shoes? Kicked off carelessly. We barely make it to the bed, and I hardly have time to admire even more of the tattoos that spider their way across Kai's muscular torso.

Goddamn, I already thought he was hot as hell. But now? I'm practically a puddle on the floor.

Kai grabs me by the hips, lifting me onto the mattress.

I grin, hooking a leg around his waist, flipping us so he lands on his back.

He laughs, breathless, wrecked already. "You just can't let me have control, can you?"

I lean down, dragging my tongue over his jaw. "You can try and take it, Pretty Boy."

Kai flips us fast, pinning my wrists above my head. His grip is unrelenting. Possessive. "You like pushing me?"

I lift a brow, smirking. "You like being pushed?"

The moment stretches between us, thick with anticipation. A sharp inhale, a lingering touch, the way his thumb drags slowly over my bottom lip, watching me like he's memorizing the way I react. The air is charged, crackling between us like the storm outside, heat pooling low in my belly with every brush of his fingers along my skin.

"You drive me fucking crazy, you know that?" His voice is a gravelly whisper, his breath hot against my lips.

A wicked grin curls my mouth as I arch into him. "Then do something about it."

He doesn't hesitate. I'm caged beneath him, pinned to the cool sheets as his body presses over mine. His hands roam—firm, knowing, possessive. Every inch of my skin is mapped with deliberate touches, leaving behind goosebumps in his wake. My pulse skitters, body thrumming with need as he drags his mouth down my neck, sucking hard enough to leave a mark.

I moan when his teeth graze my collarbone, my fingers threading into his hair, tugging. He rewards me with a low growl before dipping lower, his lips trailing a path between my breasts, down the center of my stomach. His rough palms slide beneath my thighs, spreading me open with a dominance that makes my breath catch.

"Fuck, you're soaked again," he murmurs, voice thick with appreciation.

A whimper spills from my lips when his mouth finally—finally—descends on me. His tongue is a tease, a slow, agonizing glide that makes my hips buck, chasing more. He grips my thighs tighter, holding me down as he works me open with his mouth, each flick and stroke of his tongue sending pleasure coiling through me. The sensation is overwhelming, pleasure blooming sharp and deep as I teeter on the edge.

"Please," I beg, breathless. "Don't stop."

He chuckles, the vibrations sending a shudder through me. "Never."

Two fingers slide into me, curling just right, pressing against that spot that makes stars explode behind my eyelids. His tongue works my clit mercilessly, his free hand gripping my hip to keep me exactly where he wants me. I can't do anything but take it—take him—ride the wave of heat tightening low in my belly until it snaps, pleasure flooding through me so fiercely I almost sob his name.

Before I can fully come down, he's flipping me onto my stomach, hauling my hips up with rough hands. His chest presses against my back, his breath warm and ragged against my ear. "I'm not done with you yet, baby."

The head of his cock presses against my entrance, slick and thick, teasing just enough to make me whine. Then he sinks in, inch by inch, stretching me so perfectly my fingers dig into the sheets. I gasp, arching back to take more, to take everything he gives me.

"Fuck, you feel so good," he groans, voice raw. "So fucking tight."

He sets a brutal rhythm, his hips slamming into mine, each thrust stealing my breath. The sound of skin against skin fills the room, punctuated by my moans and his curses as he takes me harder, deeper.

My face presses into the cool sheets with every thrust, but I don't mind at all. I could suffocate this way and I would go willingly.

His fingers dig into my hips, keeping me exactly where he wants me, and the feeling of being completely at his mercy sends me spiraling closer to the edge again.

A hand snakes around my throat, tilting my head back so his lips can brush my ear. "Come for me again. I want to feel you shake."

A sharp snap of his hips and I break—shattering around him, my body tightening like a vice as pleasure overtakes me. He follows with a guttural moan, burying himself deep as he finds his own release, his grip tightening as we both come undone together.

We collapse in a tangle of limbs, our breaths ragged, sweat-slicked bodies still pressed together.

His arms tighten around me, pulling me close, and I revel in the feeling of being completely wrecked, completely his.

Kai groans, rolling his hips against mine, bare skin sliding against bare skin. "Fuck, you're gonna kill me."

I moan, arching up against him, rolling my hips in return. "Then shut up and die happy."

I walk to the bathroom and pee. The last thing I need after tonight is a UTI, and we're having a *lot* of sex. I hear him talking in a muffled voice in the other room.

Probably talking to one of those thirsty bitches from the bar, planning his next hookup.

I return to the bedroom and plop back down on the bed where he lazily pulls me into the crook of his armpit, acting casual.

No need to be jealous, Dylan. You have no claim to this man. This is just one night of crazy fun.

After a long moment, he chuckles against my skin. "Round two—well, technically, round three?"

I laugh, tilting my head to meet his smirking gaze. "What did you have in mind?"

His fingers skim lazily over my thighs, promising more. "Oh, I think you know."

Kai doesn't hold back. He wrecks me, and I wreck him right back.

The hotel furniture doesn't survive. The lamp crashes to the floor. The headboard slams against the wall. Sheets are tangled, twisted, hanging half off the bed.

I'm loud.

And Kai? He eats up every fucking noise I make. "That's right, baby. Let them fucking hear you."

Every surface is fair game. Against the wall. On the bed, the sheets twisted beneath us. Against the dresser, my fingers digging into the edge for balance.

Kai pulls me onto his lap, guiding me down onto him, his hands gripping my ass. I gasp, nails digging into his shoulders. "That's it. Ride me, Trouble."

I take control. I grind down, rolling my hips, watching his jaw go tight, his eyes locked on mine as my pussy slams down over and over again onto his rock-hard cock, my breasts bouncing wildly.

His fingers dig in deeper, matching my pace, guiding me, slamming me down onto his cock.

"You feel so fucking good," I moan.

"Mmmhmm, and you're taking me so deep, fuck—"

I move faster, my head tipping back, completely lost in it.

Kai watches me, his lips parting, his grip tightening, his body tensing. He groans, a dark, wrecked sound. "Fuck, baby. You're gonna make me—"

And then he flips us onto the bed, pinning my wrists down again. "Not yet."

His voice is gritted, strained, on the edge. "I'm not fucking done with you."

He slides back into me and drives into me hard, deep, relentless. The bed creaks, shakes, threatens to collapse beneath us.

He swings my legs over his shoulders and I can't help but stare at his girth as he pounds me with his full length.

I can't breathe. Can't think. Every thrust sends me closer to the edge.

Kai unwraps my ankles from around his neck and I rewrap them around his lower back. He grips my chin, forcing me to look at him. "You wanted me to take control, didn't you?"

I can barely form words. "Yes—fuck, yes—"

Kai groans, thrusting deeper. "Then take it."

Another orgasm rips through me, my body arching, shaking, breaking. I cry out his name, not caring who hears.

Kai follows seconds later, his grip on me unrelenting, his mouth buried against my neck as he loses himself completely.

We're both wrecked. Ruined.

He collapses beside me, dragging a hand through his hair. "Holy shit."

I laugh, breathless, staring at the ceiling. "Yeah. That was… something."

The room is a disaster. Sheets lay twisted on the floor. One of the pillows has somehow made its way across the room. The nightstand is tilted sideways.

Kai turns his head toward me, watching me with something unreadable. Then he smirks. "We should do that again."

I laugh, rolling onto my side. "You say that like there was a chance we were done."

His smirk returns. "Fuck, Trouble. I'm never gonna get enough of you."

I stand up and walk in the general direction of the bathroom door. I barely have time to gasp before I'm pressed up against it, his hands already all over me again, his mouth devouring mine with the kind of hunger that feels insatiable.

Kai's lips crash against mine, still tasting of whiskey and satisfaction, but the hunger hasn't faded. If anything, it's worse now—like having me twice already only made him greedy. His fingers dig into my hips, dragging me flush against him, his body already hard, already wanting.

"You still have energy left to run that smart mouth?" he murmurs against my lips, his breath warm, teasing.

I laugh, breathless, my legs wrapping around his waist. "You're the one who's still trying to prove something, Pretty Boy. Shouldn't you be wrecked by now?"

His smirk is sharp, dangerous. "Oh, baby. I don't get tired of you. Never could."

That's all it takes. He spins, carrying me across the room before tossing me onto the mattress again. The second my back hits the sheets, he's on me with an urgency that makes my pulse spike.

His mouth is on my throat, my breasts, dragging lower, spreading fire in his wake. When his tongue flicks over my clit, I nearly arch off the bed. "Oh, fuck—"

"Not so mouthy now, are you?" he murmurs, his voice dark amusement against my skin.

I barely manage a glare before he slides two fingers into me again, curling them just right, his tongue working me over with merciless precision. My moans are shameless, desperate. My hands fist in his hair, pulling, pushing, urging him closer. He takes it as encouragement, groaning into me as he doubles his efforts.

It doesn't take long. The pleasure tightens, spirals, and then I'm shattering, my legs trembling, my cry muffled as I bite my own lip to keep from screaming.

Kai moves up my body, his mouth capturing mine. "You're gonna take every inch of me," he murmurs against my lips, positioning himself between my thighs. "And then you're gonna beg for more."

I don't get a chance to respond before he thrusts into me

again, filling me to the hilt in one brutal motion. My nails rake down his back, my body arching to take all of him. He groans, burying himself deep, his grip on my hips bruising as he sets a relentless rhythm.

"Fuck, you feel so good," he grits out. "So goddamn tight. You were made for my cock, weren't you?"

I can't even argue, can barely think past the pleasure slamming through me. All I can do is meet his thrusts, let him take, take, take until I'm nothing but sensation. He grips my chin, forcing my eyes to his, his expression wild, possessive.

With each thrust, he slams his full length into me. He varies his pace, angling his body so he rubs against my clit with every stroke.

"Say my name," he demands, his pace quickening.

"Kai," I gasp, barely able to form the word.

"Louder."

I cry it out as I come again, my body clenching around him, dragging him over the edge with me. He follows with a guttural groan, his thrusts stuttering as he spills, his weight collapsing over me.

We lay there, breathless, sweat-slicked, completely wrecked.

"Jesus Christ," I finally manage, voice hoarse. "I think you actually broke me."

Kai chuckles against my neck, his breath warm. "You're welcome."

I swat at his shoulder, making him laugh before he rolls off me, stretching out beside me on the bed. We're both a mess—hair tousled, skin flushed, our bodies still tangled in cooling sweat.

A knock at the door interrupts the moment.

Kai groans, dragging himself up. "That better be food, or I'm kicking them out."

I prop myself up on my elbows as he pulls on his jeans, walking to the door. Moments later, he returns with a tray of room service—burgers, fries, and a bottle of whiskey. "I figured we'd need to refuel," he smirks, setting it on the bed.

Oh, so that's *who he was talking to on the phone.*

I feel sheepish for jumping to conclusions earlier.

We eat naked under the covers, flipping through terrible late-night television, mocking reality show contestants and taking shots of whiskey between bites. It's ridiculous. It's perfect.

Kai groans, gesturing at the screen while I steal a fry from his plate and dip it in ketchup. "This man just said, *'I came here to find my best friend,'* and I swear to God, if he says he's 'emotionally mature' next, I'm throwing the remote. Or if they say—"

"—for the right reasons." I finish his sentence.

We look at each other and I nearly choke on my whiskey, and we both crack up laughing. "You know the script by heart, huh?"

"I have been personally victimized by this show. Every season. Every time."

I narrow my eyes. "Wait. Are you telling me you actually watch *Love Is Blind*?"

He scoffs. "Excuse me, I don't *watch* it. I *study* it."

I gasp dramatically. "Oh my god. Are you as obsessed with the gold goblets as I am?"

Kai sits up, eyes wide. "Thank you! Why do they drink *everything* out of them? Wine? Water? Orange juice? It's like the producers made a bulk purchase and now refuse to let them use normal cups. I get it's so they can chop the scenes up without the drink levels going up and down but it's like wow."

I point at him with a fry. "And have you noticed how they never fill them up on-screen but people always have a drink? Like, do they have a Goblet Refilling Goblin running around off-screen?"

Kai looks almost reverent. "You're the only person who's ever understood me."

I clutch my chest. "This is the safest I've ever felt."

He throws his head back laughing, then smirks at the TV.

"What's your stance on the whole *'I knew from the moment I heard their voice'* thing?"

I roll my eyes. "Delusion. Pure delusion. They talk through a wall for three days and suddenly they're planning their kids' names?"

He grins. "Right? And don't even get me started on the guys who propose just because they're afraid of going home early. They act like it's a job interview."

"Exactly! 'I really connected with you, but I also connected with Rachel and Stephanie, and I just feel like… my heart is telling me… that Rachel is the better fit for my brand.'"

Kai groans. "Ugh, the ones who think they're influencers already? They're my Roman Empire."

I burst out laughing and swipe a fry from his plate. "Okay, tell me something embarrassing."

He narrows his eyes playfully. "I don't get embarrassed."

I smirk. "Bullshit."

Kai sighs dramatically, then grins. "Fine. When I was fourteen, I had a crush on my math tutor. I wrote her a love letter. It had poetry. Bad poetry."

I gasp. "Please tell me it included something about 'the sum of your love completing my equation.'"

His face contorts. "I wish I was that clever. No, it was more like, 'Your eyes shine like numbers on a calculator screen. And my favorite number is 8008.'"

I shriek with laughter. "Oh my god, stop. That's iconic."

"It was a crime. And my mom still has the letter."

I nearly spit out my drink. "No."

"Oh, yes. She keeps it in a *scrapbook.*"

I cover my mouth, wheezing. "Oh my god. Did your tutor go out on a date with you?" I ask, knowing the answer and feeling the need to torment him anyway.

"No way. I never saw her again after that." Kai groans and flops back on the pillows. "I regret everything."

I grin, leaning down to kiss him. "No, you don't."

His hands slide up my back, pulling me closer. "No. I really don't."

The laughter fades, the whiskey buzz warm and lazy between us. Kai sets his empty glass aside, then turns to me, his gaze darkening. "You ready for another round, Trouble?"

I pretend to think about it, then smirk. "You sure you can keep up?"

And just like that, *Love Is Blind* and bad poetry are forgotten.

Kai growls, moving fast—rolling me onto my stomach, pinning my wrists above my head. "Oh, I'm gonna wreck you."

And he does.

This time, it's slower. Deep, devastating thrusts that leave me gasping, begging. His hand slides down, pressing between my thighs, his fingers stroking as he fucks me senseless. His voice is a low rasp against my ear, filthy words spilling over my skin, unraveling me completely.

"You love this, don't you?" he taunts. "Being pinned down, used, fucked until you can't think straight?"

I whimper, pressing back against him. "Yes."

He grins against my shoulder, his pace quickening. "Then take it."

I do. I take every deep, punishing thrust, every filthy word, until my body shatters again, pulling him over the edge with me.

When it's over, we collapse together, tangled and breathless.

"Okay," I pant, voice wrecked. "Now I think you've actually broken me."

Kai laughs, pressing a kiss to my shoulder. "Good."

CHAPTER 16

DYLAN

I lie on my back, still catching my breath, still riding the aftershocks. My body feels wrecked, spent, completely ruined in the best way possible. Every muscle loose, every nerve still thrumming, like I've been taken apart and put back together differently.

Beside me, Kai is sprawled out, one arm draped over his forehead. His chest rises and falls, still heaving from everything we just did. The cocky smirk he always wears? Nowhere in sight. Instead, he looks... relaxed. Unfiltered. *Real.*

The silence between us is thick. Not uncomfortable. Just... heavy.

The kind of silence that carries weight. Meaning.

I should say something. Make a cocky remark to lighten the mood. Tell him he's welcome for the best night of his life.

But I don't.

Instead, I just watch him.

Watch the way his brows furrow slightly, lost in thought. Watch the way his fingers twitch against the sheets, like he wants to reach for something but doesn't know what. Watch the way his lips part like he's about to say something, only to close them again.

This is the first moment we've had where we're not devouring each other. And it feels… *dangerous.*

Kai exhales sharply, dragging his fingers through his messy hair. His voice comes out lower, rougher than before. "You remind me of home."

I blink, turning my head toward him. "What?"

His jaw tightens slightly, like he didn't mean to say it out loud.

I keep watching him, waiting. My heart suddenly beats too fast, too hard.

After a moment, he lets out a short, breathless laugh—the self-deprecating kind. "Forget it. I don't know what I was saying."

"No." My voice comes out firm, steady. "Say it."

He hesitates. His fingers start tracing absent patterns over my bare stomach. Circles, lines, a rhythm I don't recognize but suddenly never want him to stop.

He exhales, eyes flicking up to the ceiling. "Back home, before rugby, before all this…" He pauses. His fingers tighten slightly against my skin, like he's grounding himself. "I had nothing but chaos. Everywhere I went, I had to fight for my place—on the field, at home, in my own fucking head."

His words hit low in my chest. Sink deep. Plant themselves there.

He turns his head toward me, eyes intense, searching. "But you…"

His voice is careful, quiet, weighted. "You feel like something familiar. Something that makes sense. Still exciting and challenging, but…" He trails off, like the words are caught in his throat. Like saying them makes them *too* real.

I don't know what to say.

Because I felt it too.

The way we push each other. Challenge each other.

The way I didn't hold back, and neither did he.

The way I've been looking for something to ground me.

And maybe... *maybe this is it.*

But that's too much. Too real.

This is a one-night stand. As simple as that. A random hookup. Nothing more.

I certainly don't need any distractions.

So I force myself to smirk, playing it off. "Damn, Pretty Boy. I didn't take you for the sentimental type."

Kai chuckles, shaking his head. "Oh, believe me, I'm not."

But something in his eyes says otherwise.

I turn onto my side, facing him fully. The sheet slips lower, but I don't care.

He watches me, waiting. For what, I don't know.

I could ask more—about his home, his family, people and things that are important to him. Dig deeper. See what else he's hiding.

But instead, I just... reach out. Drag my fingers through his messy hair, nails scratching lightly against his scalp. I feel the way his breath hitches, just for a second.

And then I press my lips to his.

Not hungry.

Not rushed.

Just... *something else.*

He lets me. Kisses me back like he doesn't want to stop. Like he doesn't know how. Like if he lets go, something will slip through his fingers that he won't get back.

And just like that, the moment is sealed.

Filed away in my memory.

A truth neither of us will ever talk about again.

Kai pulls me against him, his arms wrapping around my waist like it's instinct. His warmth sinks into my skin, his breathing slowing, steadying.

I drift off to sleep in his arms.

And for the first time in a long time, I don't feel adrift.

CHAPTER 17

DYLAN

When I wake, it's still the middle of the night. I'm face-down in the mattress, my body completely spent.

Still buzzing, still tingling, but too wrecked to move.

I tilt my head to the side.

Beside me, Kai is stretched out, his breathing steady but heavy, one arm flung over his face. As if sensing I'm awake, Kai opens his eyes and gazes at me.

Neither of us speak.

Not because we don't have anything to say—but because we just obliterated each other.

The entire room still smells like sweat, sex, and sin. Sheets half on the bed, half on the floor.

Kai is the first to shift, glancing over at me. "You good over there, Trouble?"

I don't lift my head. Don't even move. I just raise one middle finger. My face still mostly buried in the pillow.

He chuckles, rolling onto his side. His fingers trail over the bare curve of my spine, featherlight, like he knows if he presses too hard, I might actually combust. "I'd be offended, but I think I literally just fucked the attitude out of you."

I turn my head just enough to smirk. "Bold of you to assume I ever run out of attitude."

He grins, pushing up onto his elbows. "Come on. Shower."

I groan, refusing to move. "Why? We're just going to get dirty again."

Kai arches a brow, grabbing my wrist and pulling me up effortlessly. "Exactly."

The moment the water turns on, steam swirls around us, making everything hazy. The contrast between the cool air from the room and the hot water against my skin is instant, my muscles sighing in relief.

I step inside first, tilting my head back, letting the heat wash over my aching body.

Kai follows a second later, crowding into my space. His hands grip my hips immediately. "Thought you were too wrecked to move."

I smirk, placing my palms against his chest. "I could still take you."

His eyes darken. His hands tighten on my waist. "You're testing me, baby." He grabs the shampoo, flipping open the cap with one hand.

I raise a brow, arms folding over my chest. "What, you moonlight as a hairdresser?"

He smirks, working the shampoo into my hair. "Nah. Just like getting my hands in it." His fingers massage my scalp, slow, methodical.

I let out a small, involuntary sound. The kind I didn't mean to make. My body fully relaxes against him.

Kai hums against my ear. "That feel good, Trouble?"

I try to regain control, not let him see how fucking good it feels. "Fuck you."

He chuckles, hands sliding down my shoulders, down my back, massaging in slow, teasing circles. "Oh, sweetheart. You already did." He rinses out my hair, but his fingers don't leave my skin. They slide down my back, over my ass, gripping, pulling me against him.

I feel how ready he is again, and it makes my thighs clench.

He presses a kiss to my wet shoulder. "You gonna let me ruin you one more time?"

I tilt my head, smirking. "You talk big for someone who still hasn't even made me beg yet."

Kai's grin presses against my skin. "Yet." His fingers slip between my legs, teasing.

I bite my lip, pressing back against him, slick with arousal. "Less talking. More proving me wrong."

He lifts my leg, positioning me just right. The water beats down, steam thickening, making everything feel surreal. Then he thrusts in deep.

I gasp, my palms slamming against the slick tile.

He grips my hips, holding me steady as he thrusts into me over and over again. "You feel so fucking good, Trouble."

I moan, my nails dragging down his back. "Fuck, Kai—"

It's not slow, not controlled.

It's needy. Desperate. Our movements fast, messy, frenzied. Both of us chasing one last high.

Kai's teeth graze my shoulder, his grip tight on my waist. "That's it, baby. Take it. Take my hard cock."

His fingers find my clit, pressing, circling.

I moan as ripples of pleasure radiate throughout my body, his ministrations on my sensitive bud making my knees weak. I know I'm close, my entire body tensing in anticipation.

"Come for me again," he commands.

And I do. I shatter, gripping the tile, body trembling.

Kai follows moments later, groaning against my throat, his body shaking.

We're both breathless. Shaking. Wrecked beyond repair.

Kai's arms wrap around me, holding me up.
My forehead rests against the tile.
His lips press against my shoulder, soft, lingering.
Like he's memorizing this moment.
Like he knows this might be the last time.
And maybe that's the worst fucking part.

CHAPTER 18

DYLAN

The steam from the shower still clings to our skin, the heat of the bathroom lingering in the air. The hotel room is thick with sex and exhaustion, a heady mix of sweat, body heat, and the faintest scent of shampoo. The sheets beneath me are tangled, damp with the imprint of us, and the distant hum of the AC barely cools the fever lingering between us.

Kai and I tumble back onto the bed, still damp, still catching our breath. His skin is warm against mine, radiating the kind of heat that seeps into my bones, making me feel heavy, lethargic.

I collapse onto my stomach again, half-buried in the pillows, my body feeling boneless, weightless. My limbs are spent, my muscles tingling with the aftermath of too many orgasms, and a contented sigh slips from my lips before I can stop it. Somewhere in the distance, I hear the faint rumble of city traffic through the hotel window, the muffled sounds of life moving on beyond these four walls.

Beside me, Kai stretches out, one arm draped over his forehead in his usual pose, the other resting low on my back.

Not pulling me in. Not pinning me down.

Just… there.

This was supposed to be a hookup.

No strings. No emotions.

Just good sex with a cocky, insufferable rugby player.

But the way Kai's fingers move absentmindedly over the curve of my spine? Slow. Thoughtless. Like he's not even aware he's doing it.

Too soft. Too intimate.

I clench my eyes shut.

No. Not happening.

I'm not catching feelings for a man I just met.

Especially not for a player like this guy.

That kind of mistake? It could only end in tears, heartache, and maybe an STD or two.

No thanks.

This is just sex. That's all it ever needs to be.

Kai shifts beside me, exhaling a slow, contented breath, and I feel it—his body aligning closer, the weight of his thigh brushing mine beneath the sheets. A second later, his arm slides lower, pulling me against him—just slightly. His body is hot, solid, too fucking comfortable.

I should move. I should roll away, keep things casual, detached.

But for one stupid, dangerous second… I don't.

His lips brush the back of my shoulder, his voice low, rough. "You okay?"

I smirk, keeping it light. "You asking if you broke me, Pretty Boy?"

Kai huffs a soft laugh, his breath warm against my skin. "Nah." His voice is teasing, but there's something else beneath it. Something quieter. "I already know you can take it."

His arm tightens around my waist. Just for a second. A quiet, absent-minded squeeze. Like he's holding on without even realizing it.

I stare at the digital clock on the nightstand. It's late.

This should be the part where I set the boundary. Where I slip out, grab my clothes, and leave before this starts feeling like more than it is.

Kai won't stop me. He's not that kind of guy.

This was just sex.

Right?

But my body betrays me. I sink into the warmth of the bed. Into the solid weight of him behind me.

My breathing slows. My eyes flutter shut.

I should leave before morning. Before this starts feeling like something it's not.

But then Kai exhales, his hand smoothing over my hip, his fingertips tracing lazy circles there.

And just like that, sleep takes me before I can make the right choice.

As slumber embraces me, my last thought is I know I should go.

But I don't.

And Kai? He holds me like I'm his without even realizing it.

This was supposed to be nothing.

But it doesn't feel like nothing.

CHAPTER 19

DYLAN

I wake slowly, relishing after the kind of deep, satisfied sleep that only comes after being thoroughly wrecked. My body feels heavy, languid, still buzzing with the remnants of exhaustion and pleasure.

The room is quiet. The city lights peek through the curtains, casting soft shadows across the tangled sheets. The distant hum of the hotel's AC fills the silence, a steady backdrop to the soft rhythm of Kai's breathing behind me.

I shift slightly, and feel it. The warmth of Kai's body, solid and steady, the slow rise and fall of his chest pressed lightly against my back. His arm, draped lazily over my waist, holding me in that absentminded way people do when they're still caught in the haze of sleep.

For a second—just one—I let myself sink into it. The feeling of belonging. Of being held without expectation. It's been too long since I've felt this. Too long since I've woken up next to someone and wanted to stay wrapped in their warmth.

I almost turn toward him. Maybe just to see if he's awake.

Maybe just to say one more thing. Maybe just to let myself have one more minute of this.

And then the weight of what this is—and what it isn't—settles in my chest.

I'm leaving in a couple of days. This was just sex.

Kai isn't my person. I don't do messy.

I don't do feelings.

Especially not with someone like him.

And if I stay? If I wake him up—if I let him pull me back under for another round?

It's going to start feeling like something it shouldn't.

I exhale quietly, gently lifting his arm. He stirs slightly, his fingers flexing against my hip, but he doesn't wake. I pause, giving myself one last selfish second to memorize this—how he looks in sleep, how he feels against me, how stupidly good it is to be tangled up in him.

Then I slip out of bed, moving silently.

My clothes are everywhere. My crop top is draped over a chair. My skirt is barely hanging onto the nightstand. My bra is… somewhere. I untwist some of the sheets and find it tangled up in them. I move quickly, pulling on my clothes, slipping my feet into my shoes, each movement practiced, mechanical. Like the routine of someone who's done this before.

Because I have.

Because this is how you keep things simple.

Still, I steal one last glance at him.

Kai is completely relaxed, his dark hair tousled, his lips slightly parted in sleep. His usual cocky smirk is gone, replaced by something unguarded, softer. He looks different like this. Less of the cocky, arrogant rugby player who infuriates me. More… human.

Still incredibly—almost unbearably—hot.

I don't let myself think too hard as I grab my things and quietly open the door.

I pause. Just for a second.

That strange, unexpected twinge settles in my stomach.

One night. No strings. That's all it was.

I repeat it to myself like a mantra. Like it'll keep me from looking back.

And then I step into the hall, closing the door behind me.

Leaving Kai sleeping, unaware that I'm already gone.

CHAPTER 20

KAI

wake slowly, my body sore in the best way. That perfect, lingering exhaustion that only comes after a night well spent. Muscles loose. Mind foggy in the best possible way. The sheets are warm, the scent of her still clinging to them—faint, but unmistakable.

My hand instinctively reaches out, fingers brushing over the sheets. Expecting warmth. Expecting her.

But there's nothing. Just cool, empty space.

I frown, my body shifting, my mind catching up too slowly. My eyes blink open, adjusting to the dim morning light filtering through the curtains. The weight of the night before still lingers, a heady mix of memory and sensation. My muscles ache in the best way, a reminder of how thoroughly I had her beneath me, around me. The way she gave as good as she got. The way she wrecked me just as much as I wrecked her.

I turn onto my back, my gaze drifting toward the other side of the bed.

No Trouble.

No trace of her at all.

For a second—a stupid, fleeting second—I wonder if I just dreamed the whole damn thing.

But then I see it.

A faint, barely-there lipstick mark on the pillow beside me. Smudged. Subtle.

The only trace of her left behind.

I stare at it. My fingers reach out, brushing over the soft imprint, like I could somehow hold onto it. Like it'll tell me something she didn't.

Like it'll fill the silence she left behind.

My lips curl into a smirk. But it's not the usual kind. Not the cocky, self-satisfied grin I usually wear after a one-night stand. This one is…different.

This isn't new.

I've had plenty of women sneak out before. Some left notes. Some texted later. Some expected more. Some wanted nothing at all…although they usually follow up for a second or third round somewhere down the line.

But Trouble? She left nothing but a kiss stain.

And a silence that feels too fucking loud.

I drag a hand down my face, exhaling slowly, staring up at the ceiling. I tell myself it's fine. That this is how it's supposed to go. No expectations. No attachments. No strings.

That's how I live.

That's how I like it.

And yet I can't shake the feeling that she's already under my skin.

That she's not just another girl who walked away.

That if I had woken up just a little earlier…

I might have asked her to stay.

And that thought? It unsettles me more than I'd like to admit.

CHAPTER 21

KAI

n the days that follow, I don't think about her.

Not really.

Not in a way that matters.

It's just—she crosses my mind. In the quiet moments. In the lulls between training, between conversations. In the spaces where my brain has nothing better to do than wander.

I shake it off. Because it was just a night.

Her name. What was it again?

I think I remember it. Something with a D.

Dylan? Yeah. That's it, I think. Dylan. That's what she said, right? Or maybe it was Darian? Or Deanne?

That's what I get for using nicknames instead of asking again. Usually, it's a trick. A way to cover my ass when I forget.

But Trouble? That one suited her. I chuckle under my breath, thinking about it. The way she gave it right back to me. The way she never gave an inch.

Her touch.

Not just the way she felt beneath me, around me. But the way she grabbed my face when she kissed me. The way she laughed at my cockiness instead of melting under it. The way she didn't fall at my feet.

She challenged me. Met me beat for beat, push for push.

She didn't want anything from me. No games. No expectations.

And now? She's gone.

I glance at my phone out of habit. But there's nothing. No number. No message. No way to track her down.

I let out a quiet laugh, shaking my head. "Well, shit."

I guess that's that.

It was just a perfect, fleeting night. The kind of night you hold onto for a little while, just because it was good. The kind of night that doesn't mean anything. The kind of night that doesn't follow you.

And yet…

She lingers.

In the scent of whiskey and perfume still faint on my sheets. In the way my fingers twitch when I think about how she fit against me. In the phantom press of her nails down my back, in the echo of her breathy moans still stuck in my goddamn head.

I tell myself I'm only thinking about her because I can't have her. Because she slipped away before I could get bored, before I could peel back the layers and find the flaws.

That's all this is.

Stop it, Kai. You barely know her. For all I know she's completely crazy. You're only obsessing over her because she's still a mystery.

My phone buzzes.

A message from home.

A reminder of the real world waiting for me. The weight of everything I left behind pressing back in, as heavy as ever.

I exhale, running a hand through my hair. I've got bigger things to deal with.

My family.

The weight of everything back home. The pressure. The expectations. The things I can't outrun forever.

This?

This was just a break. A distraction. Something to burn through the chaos in my head for one night. That's all it ever was.

And so, I do what I do best.

I let it go.

At least, I try to.

CHAPTER 22

DYLAN

The morning air is crisp, clean. The scent of damp grass, sweat, and fresh-cut turf settles deep in my lungs. A familiar smell. A grounding one. The scent of routine, of control. Of everything I can count on.

Around me, teammates lace up their cleats, stretch, talk in low murmurs. The sound of home. The steady thud of a ball against the ground. The distant whistle of our coach barking out orders.

I stand on the field, a rugby ball gripped between my hands, rolling it between my fingers, my muscles still warm from stretching. My body is still sore from the weekend.

But not from rugby.

From him.

From Kai.

I refuse to let my brain go there.

I squeeze the ball tighter, my knuckles white around the leather. Focus. Stay sharp. There's no room for distractions here.

"Alright, let's move!" My coach's voice cuts through the fog in my head. "Warm-up drills, five minutes!"

I inhale sharply, exhaling through my nose.

No distractions. That's what I told myself before I visited the club's facility. That's what I need to remember now.

I get into formation, falling into the rhythm of the game, muscle memory taking over. Quick, precise passes fire between us. My fingers sting slightly from the repeated impact, but I welcome it.

The ball slaps against my palm, the rhythm steadying me.

This is what I know.

This field. This game.

Not him.

Not his hands on me.

Not his voice in my ear, rough and teasing, his breath against my skin.

I force the memory away, tightening my grip on the ball, sending another pass flying down the line.

The whistle blows. Four sets of 50-meter sprints.

I dig in, launching forward. The grass gives beneath my cleats, my legs burning as I push harder, faster. Lungs tightening. Heart pounding. A clear head.

This is what I do. What I've always done. Run. Push. Fight.

I try to outrun the memory of his body against mine.

The sprints bleed into drills. Tackling. Scrumming. I brace against the pack, every muscle locked tight. Bodies collide, push, fight for dominance. A controlled battle of strength and will. Just like that night.

Just like *him*.

I grit my teeth, drive forward. My heart pounds. My arms strain.

More.

Harder.

More.

The whistle shrieks, the pack breaks apart. I wipe sweat from my forehead, inhaling deeply, letting the air cool my skin, my thoughts.

One of my teammates grins, nudging me. "Damn, Dylan. You got something to prove?"

I force a smirk, shake out my arms. "Always."

But the truth?

I'm not just competing against myself.

I'm competing against the ghost of a night I refuse to let mean anything.

Coach calls for a water break. I jog to the sideline, grabbing my bottle, tilting my head back as I take a long pull of water.

The field stretches out before me. My future.

I exhale sharply, steadying myself.

One night. No strings.

I'm here for rugby.

That's all that matters.

And yet... my body still remembers. My skin still burns in places his hands have never touched in the light of day.

I shove it down. Swallow it whole.

And I walk back onto the field.

CHAPTER 23

DYLAN

I read the email for the third time. The words blur for a second, but I already know what they say.

The professional club I trained with? They want me.

Not just as a player. As assistant captain.

The title hits harder than expected.

I expected a contract offer. I didn't expect a leadership role right out of the gate.

This is better than I hoped for.

Everything I've worked for.

Everything I wanted.

And yet something still feels unsettled deep inside me.

I grab my phone, type out my acceptance email.

My finger hovers over the send button.

A moment of hesitation.

For no reason at all.

This is what I wanted. This is why I went to the camp. This is why I've been training harder than ever.

One night. No strings. Nothing to do with all of this.

I take a deep breath and press send.

———

Later, the bar is packed. My teammates surround me, shouting toasts over clinking glasses. The room is loud, buzzing with energy, laughter spilling over the hum of background music.

Someone buys another round. A fresh pint slides into my hand. Cheers ring out as beer sloshes over the rim, foaming and golden.

My teammate, Jess, slings an arm around me, grinning. "Dylan-fucking-Porter, assistant captain! Look at you, climbing the ranks already."

Another teammate, Liv, raises a brow, smirking. "So? How was the camp? Anyone interesting over there?"

The question catches me mid-sip.

I pause. Just for a fraction of a second.

Kai's face flashes through my mind. The way he looked at me in the dark. The way his fingers traced lazy circles on my hip like he didn't even realize he was doing it. The way he smirked like he had me all figured out.

I swallow, forcing a smirk, rolling my eyes. "Other than the best rugby training I've ever had? Not much to report."

Liv watches me for a beat too long, like she's weighing my answer, trying to decide if she believes me. Then she shrugs, turning back to the conversation. No one pushes. No one asks again.

I let the noise and laughter drown out the memory.

I keep Kai folded away.

A distant thing.

Not a mistake. Not something I regret.

Just... *mine.*

A night that existed outside of reality. A memory I'll never share.

The drinks keep coming, and the night stretches on, laughter and celebration a steady pulse around me. My chest swells with something that should be pure pride, untainted by anything else.

This is what I wanted. A future waiting for me. A new team. A new title. And no distractions.

That's what matters.

Or at least that's what I tell myself.

CHAPTER 24

KAI

The world narrows the second I step onto the field.

It always does.

Rugby is simple. Straightforward. You don't have to think—you just *do*.

Hit first. Run hard. Find the space. Score the try.

It's muscle memory. The only thing that's ever made sense. When everything else in my life feels complicated, rugby is the one place I know exactly what I'm supposed to do.

But today?

Today, my focus is off. *Really off.*

The whistle blows. The ball moves. My body reacts like it always does—pure instinct, driving forward, muscles locking into the brutal rhythm of play. I hit hard, slam into my opponents like it's the only thing tethering me to the present. The crunch of bodies colliding, the sting of turf scraping against my legs—it should settle me. It usually does.

But my head isn't here.

It's on a rooftop, in an alleyway, in a dimly lit hotel room.

It's in the curve of her back as she arched into me. In the sharp gasp that slipped from her lips when I sank my teeth into the soft skin of her shoulder. In the way she fucking *dared* me to give her more.

My fingers flex, gripping the fabric of my jersey like I can squeeze the memory out of my head. *Not the time, mate.*

I shake it off, scanning the field, repositioning. The play shifts. I move with it, shoving back the nagging pull of memory, the ghost of her still imprinted on my skin.

A body flies past me—too fast. I react on instinct, tracking the movement. An opponent makes a break, his legs pumping, aiming for a gap that isn't there. I step into his path, bracing for impact. The collision is solid, satisfying. His momentum dies against my chest, and he stumbles back, barely managing to stay on his feet.

I hear him swear under his breath before he shoves at my chest, a smirk curling at his mouth.

"Little tense today, are we mate?" he sneers. *"What, bad night?"*

I clench my jaw, rolling my shoulders like I can shake off the weight pressing into me.

If only he fucking knew.

I don't give him the satisfaction of a response. Just reset, feet planted, waiting for the next phase of play.

The game moves on. The roar of teammates, the heavy thud of boots against grass, the sharp calls cutting through the air.

I move with them. But my thoughts keep slipping.

Back to *her.*

Back to the way she pulled me in like she already knew I'd lose myself in her. The way her fingers dug into my back when I pushed her over the edge. The way she looked at me afterward —half-lazy, half-dazed, like I'd left a mark she hadn't been expecting.

It should've been like any other hookup. I should've forgotten her name by now. But instead, I keep catching myself reaching for my phone like I might find a message from her.

Even though we never exchanged numbers.

I tell myself it was just a one-night stand. Just *really good sex.* That's all.

So why the hell do I still feel like I can smell her perfume on my skin?

CHAPTER 25

DYLAN

I sit in the salon chair, staring at myself in the mirror. The lights are bright, clinical, making my skin look paler than usual. The stylist hovers behind me, waiting. The faint hum of blow dryers and quiet chatter fill the air. But I can't bring myself to say the words just yet.

My hair is still vibrant. Still wild. Still holding the streaks of color from that night.

The last visible trace of my recklessness.

The only evidence that Kai ever existed in my world.

I run a hand through it, exhaling slowly. It doesn't fit anymore. It doesn't feel like who I'm supposed to be now.

It was just a whim, anyway. An impulsive decision. Something out of character. Like I was meant to take on another persona—just for a brief time. A fleeting version of me that belonged to neon lights, fast hands, and the kind of raw, unfiltered pleasure that had no business following me into the real world.

Like Kai and I only existed in some alternate reality. A

moment that was an aberration, an anomaly. Something that was never meant to follow me.

But it did.

Every time I see the streaks of color in the reflection, I remember the press of his mouth against my throat, the way his hands felt gripping my hips. The way his voice—low, rough, teasing—made my whole body burn.

I swallow hard, pushing the memory down, down, down.

"So, what are we thinking?" The stylist's voice pulls me out of my thoughts. She offers me an easy smile in the mirror, but there's a flicker of curiosity in her eyes, like she can tell this is more than just a haircut.

I lift my gaze, meeting my own eyes in the mirror. "Cut it. And dye it closer to my natural color."

The stylist tilts her head. "Cut all of it?"

"Not all of it." I shift in the chair. "Just… make it cleaner. Natural."

She nods, draping the cape over me. The scissors glint under the salon lights.

Then the first lock of hair falls to the floor. Then more. Bright magenta. Teal. Lock after lock disappears, along with who I was that night.

Gone.

I watch the colors disappear, piece by piece.

I tell myself it's just hair.

It doesn't mean anything. I'm not getting rid of a memory. I'm just making a smart choice. I'm stepping into a new phase of my life. One with structure. With purpose. With no space for ghosts of a night that was never supposed to mean anything.

I can't be the girl who made reckless choices in dark alleyways.

I can't be the girl who let a stranger ruin her for anyone else.

The stylist spins the chair around. I barely recognize myself.

The bright colors? No more.

What's left is shorter, much more natural.

More put-together. More serious.

More like the professional sportswoman I need to be.

That night was just a detour.

It didn't mean anything.

I stand, pay, step out onto the street. The air is crisp, the city alive around me. I feel lighter. Freer. Like I've cut more than just my hair. Like I've severed something intangible—something that has been lingering in my chest since the moment I walked away from him.

The past is behind me.

And yet, I have no idea it's about to collide with me again.

And this time? I won't be able to pretend it didn't matter.

CHAPTER 26

KAI

A FEW MONTHS LATER

lean back in my chair, cracking my neck, exhaustion settling deep into my bones. The room is quiet, the only glow coming from my laptop screen. The official roster for the upcoming season stares back at me.

New transfers. Rising talent. Leadership appointments.

I skim through it absently, barely paying attention. My mind is elsewhere.

Back home.

Family.

The stress I've been drowning in.

My eyes flick past the assistant captain announcement—then snap back.

Dylan Porter.

Something stirs deep in my chest. The name is familiar. But it doesn't immediately click.

It's like a song lyric on the tip of my tongue. Something I should know. Something that should mean something.

I frown, clicking on the headshot next to the name.

I study the photo. The sharp jawline. The piercing confidence in her gaze. The way she carries herself—strong, unshaken, ready for war.

A slow, nagging déjà vu creeps in.

I know that face.

But…why does it feel different?

My brain tries to place her, but the image won't stick. It's like looking at a puzzle with missing pieces.

Like I should know her. Like I should remember.

But I don't.

I exhale sharply, dragging a hand down my face. It's just the stress. Too much on my plate. Too many sleepless nights. Too much pressure from every angle.

My heart kicked a little harder when I saw her name—but that doesn't mean anything.

Right?

It's just another player. Just another teammate.

I don't know any female rugby players other than the ones at this club, and it looks like she's coming in from out of town. She probably just reminds me of someone.

Maybe a player I've gone up against in a match. Maybe a face I saw in a crowded bar, in the blur of too many drinks and half-forgotten nights. Maybe nothing at all.

I shake my head, trying to clear it, trying to convince myself it's just a coincidence. But something lingers. Something won't let go.

I shut the laptop. Push it from my mind.

It's nothing.

But deep down, in the quiet part of me I don't listen to…

I know.

It's not nothing.

That name. That face.

I've seen her before.

And fate?

I can't help but think that fate isn't done with us yet.

Ready for more rugby action? Check out the next book in this series, Rucked!

Ready for some RH/why choose, this time with surfing? Check out my Blood and Sand series.

Enjoyed Quick Tap? Sign up here to get early announcements about new releases, giveaways, bonus scenes, opportunities to join my ARC team for future releases, and more!

Heidi's other books:

Blood and Sand (Dark Why Choose Mafia Romance)

• Sea of Snakes (Book 1)

• Sea of Sinners (Book 2)

• Sea of Rage (Book 3)

• Sea of Pain (Book 4)

• Sinners, Rage & Pain: The Brixton Trilogy (Books 2, 3 and 4)

• Sea of Demons(Book 5)

• Sea of Redemption(Book 6)

Burn It All Down Duet (dark stalker romance x psychological/domestic thriller)

• Volcano of Pain (Book 1)

• Beautiful Terror (Book 2)

C(r)ouch Bind Set Series (rugby why choose sports romance)

• Rucked

Standalones

• Pretty Lovely Lies (FBI/mafia romance, single parent, international)

• Ruthless Choices (romantic horror)

- F*CKBOYS (dark revenge romance, second chance, enemies to lovers)

  - Marco: Hearts of the Underworld (dark mafia romance)

Billionaire's Takeover Collection
- Irreversible Decision
- Compelling Proposal
- Love Merger
- The Billionaire's Takeover Collection (all 3 of the above)

Novellas
- Love in a Seedy Motel Room

Sign up for my newsletter here for the latest on new releases, promos, giveaways and events!

Join me on social media:
    Facebook: @heidistarkauthor
    Instagram: @heidistarkauthor
    TikTok: @heidistark_author
    Bluesky: @heidistarkauthor

Website: https://heidistarkauthor.com

ABOUT THE AUTHOR

Heidi Stark writes contemporary dark romance with a twist of danger, desire, and the occasional sports scandal.

Known for her badass heroines and irresistibly morally grey men, Heidi has captivated readers with 20+ titles, including the gripping *Blood and Sand* series and the devastatingly pitch-black *Burn It All Down Duet*.

Originally hailing from the lush landscapes of New Zealand, Heidi now calls the U.S. home, where she shares her creative chaos with her feline sidekick, Fang.

When she's not crafting heart-pounding stories, Heidi is a whirlwind of energy—hitting up barre classes, devouring true crime podcasts, dabbling in roller derby, people-watching, or indulging in her guilty pleasure: reality TV binges. Always on the hunt for inspiration, she's probably plotting her next book—or her next travel adventure.

Dark, daring, and deliciously addictive—Heidi's world is one you'll never want to leave.

ACKNOWLEDGMENTS

Thanks as always to my fantastic editor, Trish, my wonderful PA, Taylor, and my beta reading team.

To everyone who demanded MORE of Dylan and the guys, who messaged me relentlessly about Kai's and her history — this one's for you. Your passion fueled mine.

Ass always, to Ed, Fang, Diamond and Pearl xoxo

And a massive shout-out to my home country of New Zealand – the breathtaking playground that sparked my rugby obsession and continues to inspire every game scene I write! LOVE YOU, AOTEAROA!